Praise for *The Wrong Side of Midnight*

"Thoroughly engrossing, Hammarberg delivers a dark, twisted tale filled with blood and hilarity! This was such a blast!

—Steve Stred, author of *Mastodon* and *Churn the Soil*

"Tackling the age-old question "what's it like to be a punk rock accordion player on LSD at an AARP-orgy that's attacked by blood sucking freaks," Hammarberg's answer is as hilarious and strangely enlightening as you could've ever hoped. A gonzo splatterfest of sardonic wit, sly observations, and blistering b-movie mayhem."

—Phil Mucci, writer/creator of *Professor Dario Bava* and *Gringo Loco*

"With his trademark razor sharp wit and gruesome storytelling, Peter Hammarberg does it again with The Wrong Side of Midnight. Fast paced and wickedly funny, I could not look away from the carnage."

—Shannon Cox, author and co-host of the *THC Library* podcast

"Beneath the insanity, sex, gore, and top-notch one-liners in The Wrong Side of Midnight, there's a constant that remains in Peter Hammarberg's writing: a touch of poetry. He's a god damn wordsmith, and I love the overlapping universes he continues to build upon."

—Justin Weingartner, illustrator at @justinwdraws, and Alan Sparklemane disciple

"Absurd. Crass. Soaked in blood and bad decisions. Think punk rock 'From Dusk Till Dawn' or 'What We Do in the Shadows' with shotguns and get ready for a bloody good time."

—Tim Mucci, author of *All-Action Classics: Tom Sawyer*, *All-Action Classics: The Odyssey*, and the horror comic *Eternal Gaze of the Sightless Void* on AdventuresUnlimited.Substack.com

The Wrong Side of Midnight

Peter Hammarberg

The Wrong Side of Midnight. Copyright 2026 Peter Hammarberg and Hammer Mountain Arts. All rights reserved. Thank you for buying an authorized edition of this book, complying with copyright laws, and supporting independent writers, artists, designers, and creators. Please note that no part of this book may be used or reproduced in any manner for the purpose of training artificial intelligence technologies or systems. No part of this publication may be used or reproduced in any manner whatsoever without the written permission of the publisher, except in the case of brief quotations embodied in critical articles and reviews.

This is a work of fiction. Names, characters, places, and incidents are products of the author's imagination, used fictitiously, and are not to be construed as real. Any resemblance to actual events, locales, organizations, or persons, living or dead, is entirely coincidental.

ISBN: 978-0-9908397-3-6

Cover and interior art by Mike Kessell
mrkessell.com

Cover design and typography by: Robert Paul Nixon
@robertpaulnixon

Special thanks to (in no particular order):

Mike Kessell, Nix, Justin Weingartner, Steve Stred, The Mystic Order of the Golden Tentacle, Espen Aukan, Shannon Cox, Krista Rosadiuk, Dom Kreep, Tim Mucci, Jason Axiom, Jonathan Porges, Madison King, Annie Stuart, Matt Perry, Alexa Colpitts, Mike Guay, Dani Shaw, Tina Walker, Kevin Incroyable, Jon Stroker, Manny Patiño, Andy Brackett, Andrea Dobbs, Diabolik LLC, Pond Maidens of New England, Crap-O-Rama, and John Noble.

For Christina, Alex, and Special Agent Cooper Dwayne "Spooky-Boy" Hammarberg (the cat). Thank you for loving me through my lows and tolerating me through my highs.

"Sleep's the mortar in which every day gets crushed
Mixed with memory and dread, desire and lust
And I'm only slightly sad to cause you all this pain
Cause some mistakes they take a whole lifetime to pay
And now there's no witness to any of my crimes
So how could anybody say I'm truly not divine?
Now I'm losing all my dreams
Let the morning come"

Dom Kreep
"I'm Losing All My Dreams"

"Immortalized by hateful lies cruelly claiming your prize
Only fangs remain to claim some fame
In the shape of wounds we can all recognize

Look what you learned, the prizes you've earned
The angels are falling with wings bent and burned
And you laughed in the shadows amused by this turn

Oblivious to the oncoming darkness and worms
The slow creeping certainty of darkness and worms"

Kevin Incroyable
"Dirty Susan"

SLUG WEEKEND
MULLET HORSE.
ALL AGES!
GRUNDEL BUSKET
09/21 @7pm
SHOEHORN
GRUNDLE BUSKET
A PROBLEM FOR YOUR
1. WE ARE GRUNDLE BUSKET
2. OLD MONEY, NEW BLOOD
3. IRON MAN DIED (FOR OUR SINS)
4. SOUP SANDWICH!
5. MOOSE KNUCKLE MASHUP
6. SACRED/SCARED
7. A PROBLEM FOR YOUR SOLUTION
8. TACO DUCK
9. ATHEIST'S PRAYER
10. NUN SMOKE
11. GUTTER GLITTER
12. THERE IS NO TITLE FOR THIS SONG
13. LAST DANCE IN THE GRAVEYARD
HONEY SLUDGE
CITIZEN SQUATCH
FALUMPTUTIOUS
GRUNDLE BUSKET
NO PARKING
LIVE AT THE
AX GRINDER
TUESDAY 11/02
$5
8pm
BECOME A BUSKETEER TODAY!
WTF is a busketeer?!!

1

"This place doesn't seem right …" Dax grunted as the Grundle Busket tour van passed the *Welcome to Pacton New Hampshire* sign.

He took his bare feet off the dashboard to the unspoken relief of Lee-Lee Allore--lead singer and current driver--who hated everyone and anyone who thought that placing one's feet upon the dashboard was fine and dandy. To her, it was the opposite: good-for-nothing sub-humans. Have some respect for the vessel that stands between destination and destiny. She ran her fingers over the stubble of the undercut that her crimson-dyed hair usually obscured when it wasn't gelled into three-foot spikes. It was her fidget, and her companion knew something was up.

"I hate feet," Lee-Lee said.

Dax, the bass player, scratched his chin through a thick, black beard and looked at her in confusion. "What does that have to do with what I said?"

"Nothing," Lee-Lee replied with a shrug. "I think putting your feet on the dashboard is a sin."

"Sorry, Anti-Tarantino," Dax chuffed and rolled his window down, causing some of the other members of the band to stir.

It was only 4:15 in the afternoon, but when you're touring as one of America's least memorable bands, you sleep when you can. Or all the time.

"The hell are we anyway?"

"Pacton, New Hampshire," Lee-Lee stated, looking around the regal-yet-curiously-desolate town square that was usually known for their tourism and high-end consumerism. "One of the most opulent and insulated towns in the Lakes Region."

"Looks like a ghost town," Mia Silver, keyboardist, groaned from the left side of the back bench. "I thought you said this town was 'an Autumnal Haven of turning leaves and old Pagan festivals'." She cleared her smoker's throat with enough force to rattle the window. "I don't see what all the hubbub is. And you could have called her Taranti*nope*, Dax."

"Number one: nobody says *hubbub*. Number two: my Uncle Lucas has a bed and breakfast here, so I figure instead of pushing all the way to Burlington, Vermont, we'd stop for the night."

Lee-Lee turned onto Main Street and the group plodded past darkened store after darkened store—each more superficial than the next. "Though, ok … I'll admit that this seems a bit suspect from what I remember as a kid."

"They going to be okay with us?" Mia asked.

"What do you mean?" Lee-Lee inquired. "Like, the band? I'm sure we'll be an inconvenience, but … I grew up here, more or less."

"No, I mean, *us*: A Chinese lesbian, a Mexican, and a …" she looked at Dax.

"As long as the next few words are going to be '*black guy*,' you can say it."

"I was going to say, 'big black man with arms like tree limbs and a massive—'"

"Don't talk about my dick, Mia. It's inappropriate." Dax shook his head.

"Why would I want to talk about that? Hello? Chinese lesbian, here!"

The shared laughter broke a bit of the tension. Lee-Lee rolled her knuckles gently on the window as she saw the town she once knew but no longer recognized.

"No…" she smiled. "We'll be fine."

Pacton, nestled in one of the larger alcoves of Lake Winnipesaukee, was a colonial town that not only withstood the tests of time and turmoil, but seemed to have thrived because of them. One of the most opulent areas in America, Pacton had always exhibited itself rather curiously. A juxtaposition of algae-riddled docks, generations-old seafood joints, and multimillion dollar dwellings, the town had never expanded and tried to keep the New England charm that granted tourists all the enchanting trappings of a quaint, small-town hideaway. As *Get Lost Magazine* once described it: "I'm so very confused, but I love it here!".

The town was decked out for Halloween—lights hung from abandoned cafes with signs that read *Thanks for a great season! See you next year!* Jack-o'-lanterns, pristine in their garishness, leered from perfectly landscaped lawns.

"Where are all the trick or treaters?" Rafael "Boom-Boom" Restrepo, the drummer, asked as he roused.

He noticed empty yard after empty sidewalk after empty street and thought it was extremely odd.

"This the only town in New England that

doesn't give a shit about Halloween? Why bother decorating then? Side note: you ever wonder why we can't book a show on Halloween? Or any holiday, for that matter? I mean, what are we even trying to sound like? Goth? Punk? Fuckin'… that gypsy shit? Our noise is all over the place!"

"True that," Bella Frank, lead guitarist, sighed from the right side of the bench. "Not that it makes a difference, though—we're *never* getting a record deal."

"Not with *that* attitude!" Dax interjected.

"Our sound is *supposed* to be … nebulous and shit!" Lee-Lee shouted in a futile attempt to shut the bullshit ouroboros down.

"One track we're singing about the existential dread of being little more than sparkplugs in rotting meat machines, and the next is a summertime anthem about how much summer sucks … then, you know, songs about … spooky shit … and love and whatever …"

Lee-Lee realized halfway through the spiel that her argument wasn't very convincing.

"For *another* thing, we have a fucking accordion player," Bella pressed her point. What kind of self-respecting goth … punk … doom—*whatever the hell we are*—band has an accordion player?"

"I also play the triangle *and* windchimes," Jessie Campbell (whatever he is) stated heroically from the back of the van.

He struggled to sit up amidst the band's equipment.

"And you look like a fucking Ren-faire Shaggy with ear gauges," Bella joked.

"T'wasn't me, m'lady."

"Wrong Shaggy, Dicknuts." Bella chuckled.

She ran her hands over her shaved head to feel the tingle of the stubble growing in. They passed under a streetlamp. Bella saw her reflection and the new Bob-omb tattoo on her neck and smiled. She was a proud, plus-sized punk-rock pixie-princess. It had taken her a long time to feel that way, and sometimes she had to fake it. Mia helps, though. Usually with reaffirmations and hand stuff. Hence why Rafael was stationed between the two.

"Nobody thought it's because we have the stupidest band name in the history of band names?" Jessie continued. "And that's including Maroon 5, Limp Bizkit, *and* Quiet Riot."

"Don't throw shade at Quiet Riot!" Rafael shouted. "What's wrong with that name?"

"You ever heard a riot that was quiet? No. Is their music quiet? No. So, like … the fuck is going on there?"

"Oh, but *Grundle Busket* is okay?" Mia interjected, lighting a cigarette, much to the ire of the lead singer. "I've been in this band for what, two years? And I still have no goddamn clue what our name means. It's not clever. It's not edgy. It's not catchy. The hell is it supposed to be?"

"Meta." Lee-Lee grunted.

"*Here* we go …" Jessie rolled his eyes.

"A grundle…" Lee-Lee began as she slowed the van down in order to get her bearings.

It had been many years since she last visited her uncle and aunt, and since then a lot had changed. Not the layout of the town, per-se, but the overall look.

"… is slang for someone's taint. And a busket, well, Dax can tell you that."

"Don't bring me into this shit," Dax stuck his head out of the window and took a deep breath of crisp autumn air through his nose.

"Too late, grundle," Mia joked.

"Fine. A *busket* is a word from 1997's crime-thriller-comedy, *Suicide Kings*, directed by Peter O'Fallon. There's a scene where Denis Leary's character—who's a hitman—is sitting at a light, when a homeless guy comes up and starts to use this shit-water rag to clean his windshield. He's just smearing dirty water all over the glass, so Leary gets out of the car and smacks the guy's bucket out of his hands, right? And—and the guy shouts 'My busket!' So, Leary like, grabs the bucket and shoves it at the homeless guy and says, 'Here's your fuckin' busket!' and pushes the guy away. It's been a while since I saw that movie, but I'm pretty sure that's how it went."

"And that, ladies and gentlemen, is why we don't have a record deal."

Mia inhaled her cigarette sharply then held the smoke until her eyes stung.

"Hey, look at that …" Rafael gestured to one of the magnificent houses. "There's no decorations except that big, red candle on the doorstep."

"I can dig it," Bella smiled. "Minimalistic. Striking. That's the perfect *come hither to yon doom* decoration."

"Yo, pass me a stink stick, Mia," Jessie said. "You already got this van funked up—I might as well join in."

"You two and those fucking cigarettes!" Lee-Lee groaned. "They're gonna kill us all!"

She turned the van left, sending the band up a steep, winding road. The setting sun shimmered enchantingly on the harbor in hues of pink and red, causing everyone to pause their ridiculousness.

"Haven't seen that in at least twelve years," Lee-Lee stated softly.

"*Mal Burro*, baby!" Jessie cheered the cigarette brand's tagline, disrupting the tranquility of the moment. "'*That's one baaaaaaaad donkey!*' Hey … anybody got a light?"

"Rub two drumsticks together, caveman," Dax chuckled.

"Don't you dare, pendejo," Rafael pointed his finger at Jessie then something caught his eye. "Hey, look! A party!"

The group drove slowly past a beautiful colonial house full of revelers in various degrees of revelry. A tour bus parked in the street had the words *Party Palace Tours* decaled on it.

"That's where we're heading after we get checked in or whatever. Maybe we can even land a gig. Finally, a Halloween show!"

"There's another red candle," Bella noticed. "What's up with that, Lee?"

"No idea, Bella," Lee-Lee shrugged. "If it happened when I was a kid, I don't remember it. Maybe Google it?"

"I haven't had service since we got to town," Bella shook her head.

"Me either," Dax stated as he attempted to eke out a high-pitched fart without it bringing friends. "This is some strange goddamn place you've dragged us to. Whoa! Stop the van a sec!"

Lee-Lee reluctantly did as asked, and the band watched a partygoer urinate on the red candle's flame. It took ten full seconds of cheap beer piss downpour to snuff the flame. The crowd cheered. A distinguished man in his sixties immediately appeared at the front door and stormed down the steps with a thunderous *toom toom toom* of his cane.

"Shit's about to go down!" Mia said with a bit more excitement than she anticipated.

The owner of the establishment pointed at the candle, then at the offender. No one in the van could hear what words were being exchanged. The younger fellow—the offender—threw his hands up in a gesture of *well, I can't un-piss it, can I?* and promptly had his testicles caved in by the brass deep sea diver helmet pommel on the proprietor's cane.

The band collectively gasped. The partygoers just laughed and carried on. The proprietor dumped the urine out and attempted to relight the candle.

It didn't work.

He then spoke into a small walkie-talkie, which caused his voluptuous, white nightgown-wearing wife to appear to the hoots of the crowd. She rushed to her husband and handed him another red candle which lit with ease. He placed the candle down in the same spot as the last and spoke to the revelers about his expectations—using the brass pommel for emphasis.

"What. The. Fuck. Did. We. Just. See?" Jessie asked.

"A straight up, one hundred percent made from concentrated GILF!" Rafael exclaimed with admiration. "We definitely need to circle back to this joint!"

"Pigs," Bella groaned. "Oh, and Lee? I think you don't know what *meta* means."

"Whatever, bish—I know my nomenclature."

"Say that five times fast. I know my nomy—I know my noméclatty … shit, I can't even say it one time slow," Rafael laughed.

"Noméclatty sounds like something a Jamaican would call you if they thought you were an asshole," Dax chuckled.

"Or a *grundle*," Jessie added, blowing smoke through his nostrils.

"You guys are hi-larious," Lee-Lee rolled her eyes. "But see? You're using grundle a lot more now that you know what it means."

"Still a stupid name," Mia dropped her

cigarette butt from her awning window.

"Hey, shut up, we're here."

Lee-Lee made a right onto the inclined driveway of her uncle's massive Victorian-style home. The band admired the wrap-around porch, steep multi-eave rooflines with grey fish scale shingles, and its many intersecting gables.

Unlike his neighbor on the opposite side of the street adjacent, Uncle Lucas didn't have a red candle outside his modest mansion.

"This place looks like a Richter scale printout," Rafael stated in awe.

"Your grandpa must be loaded!" Jessie hooted.

"Yeah, he kinda is," Lee-Lee admitted.

"So, like, why are we all stuck in this shit-ass van, living off gas station jerky and Über Düche energy drinks?" Dax asked, a bit more irritated than he had any right to be.

"He's my uncle, not my grandpa—and that doesn't mean the rest of the family is rich." Lee-Lee answered with the right amount of *screw you.*

"Well, maybe he can toss a few bucks to help his sweet, itty-bitty baby niece out." Jessie said.

"Couldn't hurt to ask," Mia shrugged.

"First off, what about my pride?" Lee-Lee said with indignation. "And second, we're already asking him to spend the night at his beautiful house without *any* kind of notice. You don't think that's not already pushing it?"

"See my previous statement," Mia said.

"See my middle finger," Lee-Lee flipped the keyboardist off.

The van came to a stop in front of the three-car garage and nearly sputtered itself off.

"We gotta fill up first thing tomorrow," Lee-Lee said more to herself than to anyone.

"When have we ever been able to fill up?" Dax asked.

"Maybe after Lee asks Big Daddy Money Bucks for some of that old, colonist money," Mia said with disdain.

"*Uncle* Money Bucks," Rafael corrected.

"What did the colonists do to you, Mia?" Dax asked.

"Google it sometime…" Mia said flatly.

"Alright, everyone," Lee-Lee turned around in her seat to address the band. "Let's squash whatever bullshit tension we've been building and focus on being the most polite, non-threatening group of people who are in simple need of a place to sleep the night, alright? No talk of colonial imperialism, or GILFs, or-or-whatever dumb shit that comes out of our mouths that I can't keep track of. Okay? Can we agree on a common purpose? Uncle Lucas can easily, and maybe rightfully, say no. We have to present ourselves in need of help—"

"—And money," Jessie interposed. The band agreed and began filing out of the van.

"Bring as much as you can carry," Dax said, hefting his rucksack over his shoulder and grabbing his bass' hardcase covered in stickers of places they've played and the bands they've played with. "This way, we looked overburdened and extra in need."

"Diabolical…" Bella smiled. "I like it."

The band gathered what they could: clothes-stuffed duffle bags and their instruments minus amplifiers. But pathetic they indeed looked when Lee-Lee pressed the doorbell. Then again. Then *again* after what seemed an eternity. Jessie looked across the street to another magnificent house that was teeming with life. The vinyl sign staked on the lawn said, '*Welcome to Guru Lightbringer Dukehouse's Annual Retreat! Namaste for a while!'*

Jessie scoffed, but noticed that the home also had that large, red candle out front.

"The fuck is a Dukehouse?" Jessie asked.

"Sounds like a pseudonym for a butthole," Dax chuckled. "Gotta evict some tenants from my Dukehouse …"

"Guys! Focus for fuck's sake!" Lee-Lee hissed.

Uncle Lucas, and Aunt Gretta finally swung the door open in anger. They were wearing bathrobes and slippers—which one would argue is typical for older folks in the evening—but they wore nothing else. Uncle Lucas struggled to keep his erection from breaching the fold in the robe.

"What is the meaning of—?" Uncle Lucas was cut short by the sight of his niece. "Lilly? Is that you?"

"Hi, Uncle Lucas … Aunt Gretta." Lee-Lee said with a meek smile. "Mind if we crash the night?"

"Bro, Unc is packing *major* sausage," Rafael said to Jessie, who looked away in awkwardness.

The band could hear moans coming from within the house. Lee-Lee tried to not put two and two together.

"You have to go! Now!" Aunt Gretta shouted. "Now!"

"There's no time, Gretta!" Uncle Lucas pressed. "Goddamn it all, Lilly, why are you here? The road should have been closed off!"

"It wasn't … I'm sorry, Uncle Lucas, we—"

"Hhhh," Uncle Lucas rubbed his brow in frustration. "What the devil is Chief Harris up to?"

"Again, I'm so sorry—*we're* so sorry for the for the intrusion. We're on our way to a gig in Vermont, and we just can't make it without some rest, and I thought—"

"'Get in—*come* in," Uncle Lucas stammered,

ushering the band inside, much to his wife's ire.

"There's so many of them!" Aunt Gretta scowled.

"We have the room and it's *Lilly!* And there's no time lef—"

A firehouse siren blared, causing Lee-Lee's Aunt and Uncle to shudder. He quickly slammed the door and locked it. He then took a deep breath and exhaled slowly, turning to his new guests.

"Alright. This isn't the best night for you to visit. I understand that you think you had no other choice, but … no … you wouldn't understand anything I was about to explain."

"Ew," Mia sneered.

"We get it, Unc," Rafael smirked. "There's an orgy going on, and you're understandably-yet unnecessarily embarrassed. I've got a thing for mature women, so if you want a hand with this silver fox, I'm your guy!"

Rafael winked at Aunt Gretta, who, despite herself, blushed.

"And I can provide the music!" Jessie exclaimed while holding up his accordion.

"Focus!" Uncle Lucas shouted. "If you are to stay here, you must, and I cannot over-emphasize *must*, adhere to what I am about to tell you. Is that clear? I need each and every single one of you to agree or get the hell out of my house right now! Goddamn it, Lilly, really."

"I'm so sorry, Uncle Lucas. We were so close, and I didn't think you'd mind."

"First! Do *not* open any doors or windows to the outside! I cannot stress this enough! Once night has fallen, you are to remain inside, and the inside is to remain shut tight! *Do* you understand? Under *no* circumstances are any of you to open a window or door that leads outside! That siren meant that we're all out of time—no second thoughts on staying here the night. Second! Do not interfere with the people who are already here. Keep to yourselves. Mister … whomever you are …"

"Rafael Restrepo, Sir. People call me Boom-Boom."

"You're correct in your assumptions, as embarrassed as it makes me. You might not want to witness what's going on, so please stay in your rooms. Let me take you to them. Love? Feel free to return to the festivities."

"This is a *mistake*, Lucas," Aunt Gretta said with a shake of her head. She grudgingly left the group to return to her Halloween debauchery.

"Lucky man, Papá," Rafael smiled.

"You don't know the half of it, young man. Now follow me."

Uncle Lucas ushered the band upstairs then down a long hallway.

"Your rooms are here. Take one for each of you, shack up, it doesn't matter, just leave the rooms on the right side of the hallway alone, as they are for our other … guests. Again, split up, stay together, I really don't care as long as you follow the rules."

"There a place we can eat?" Dax asked, reshouldering his rucksack. "Seemed like the only show in town was that house party a few blocks down and whatever shit is going on across the street from here."

"Yeah, the party looked wild. Chicks, dancing, drinks, and boozers pissing on candles …" Jessie added.

"What happened to the candle?" Uncle Lucas asked urgently. There was a palpable anxiety in his voice.

"Some dipshit doused the flame, and some abuelo came out and clubbed the dude's junk with his cane!" Rafael said.

The panic in Uncle Lucas' voice remained. "What of the candle?"

"Old dude had his hot wife get another."

"What actually *is* the deal with the candles?" Bella asked. "This is just about a ghost town except for a party and a couple of red candles. I don't know what's going on across the street from here, but they have one too. The other place we saw with one didn't have anything going on."

"The candles are a time-honored tradition. Anyway, these are your rooms. If you take a left at the bottom of the back stairs, you'll find the kitchen. Eat what you want. It's fine as long as you follow the rules."

"What if we break the rules?" Mia asked, trying to test her reluctant host's boundaries.

"Have you ever put your fingers in a blender and switched it on?"

"No," Mia answered with a bit of sass. "That's stupid."

"Right—so is disobeying the rules." Uncle Lucas dismissively waved his left hand.

"That's not an actual reason, though," Dax shrugged and crossed his thick arms.

"Fine," Uncle Lucas growled with stern eyes. "You lot fuck this up, and we'll all be eviscerated by ancient vampires. That a *better* reason?"

"Homeboy is in the Halloween spirit!" Jessie laughed. "We'll play by your rules, as long as you're not some Scooby Doo villain."

"I assure you I am not. I want to see sunrise too. Go and eat, and do not go to the other side of the house. Just pick a room and stay until morning, then be on your way."

"Seriously, Uncle Lucas, I'm really sorry for the inconvenience," Lee-Lee said with authentic shame.

Uncle Lucas gave her a heartfelt—but awkward—hug.

"This isn't ideal. And *completely* the worst timing, but you are family, and I will do what I can. Seriously, though, it never occurred to you to call in advance?"

"I'm … living … my vida loca," Lee-Lee stated with a noticeable lack of conviction.

"Whatever the case, you've all heard what you've needed to hear to survive the night *without* charge, correct?"

Uncle Lucas stared at each member of Grundle Busket until they uttered an agreement. They were eager to acquiesce once he said *without charge*. He sighed deeply.

"Very well, then. See you all in the morning. Pay no attention to the screams."

"You mean moans," Bella sneered with a palpable ick in her voice."

"Have fun at the orgy!" Rafael saluted. "Lemme know if you need me to tag in!" Uncle Lucas shook his head and walked away.

"Wait …" Dax turned to his friends with a cocked eyebrow. "Did he say *survive*?"

2

"I've raided a few … dozen kitchens in my day," Jessie said with a mouthful of cold, leftover shrimp fettuccine. "But this one is by *far* superior."

He took a large gulp of white wine despite being a fan of red. He didn't want to come across as an uneducated mooch, but as a high-class one. Pairing is everything.

"You alright, Boom-Boom?" Dax asked the drummer, who was leaning on the kitchen doorframe listening to the sounds of ecstasy billowing from the other side of the house.

"I wanna be in the thick of that sweet sound, Dax," Rafael admitted. "There's nothing like the soft crash of a group of naked bodies to show you just how good life is."

"Two of those bodies I'm related to, perv!" Lee-Lee grimaced.

She pushed her mostly eaten plate of Wagyu steak and garlic-seared string beans away. Despite the evening's fare being constructed from leftovers, the band couldn't recall the last time they've eaten so well. If ever.

"Hey, love is love," Rafael stated before walking over to the kitchen island and sensually slurping the last of Jessie's fettuccini. "But lust is an entirely different beast. You know what? I'm going down there."

"Me too!" Jessie agreed, holding his accordion case high.

"Ugh! Oh my god, you two!" Lee-Lee groaned in disgust at the thought of her bandmates sweating to the oldies.

"The hell are you bringing your accordion for, weirdo?" Mia asked, knowing fully well that she would not like the answer.

"Lucinda never leaves my side, and older folks love smashing pissholes to oompah music. So, I shall provide!"

"You chucklefucks are going to get us kicked out." Lee-Lee placed her face in her hands in defeat.

Rafael and Jessie scurried from the kitchen as the rest took care of clean up. Lee-Lee couldn't help but notice Dax's lingering looks. He wanted one of two things: Sex, or a long, prickly conversation.

"I know that look," Mia smiled. "Bella and I will leave you be."

"It's nothing—what are you even talking about?" Dax asked completely off guard.

"We're not as stupid as you wish we were, big boy. We'll see you in the morning."

"And thanks for the hookup, Lee," Bella added. "Been a while since I felt human. I think a shower will seal the deal. Goodnight, weirdos!"

The girls took each other's hands and left the room. It seemed as though they took the temperature with them.

"Feels like it's suddenly freezing in here," Lee-Lee mentioned, successfully finishing her meal despite her prior disgust.

"Maybe I can warm you up?" Dax asked timidly.

One of the things that drew Lee-Lee to Dax was the way his personality contradicted his stature. His looks would make you think he would be better suited storming a castle, but his actions would marginalize him as *sensitive*. Underneath the tattooed muscles was the heart of a poet. Lee-Lee would relish in the discomfort Dax would have at that very phrase.

Heart of a poet. Gag.

"I don't think that's a great idea, *Darrion*," Lee-Lee said, knowing that Dax's true name was a trigger for him.

"I just wanted to talk about what happened, *Lilly*." Dax snapped back.

The two stood in silence for an eternity of forty-five seconds, then Dax left Lee-Lee alone among the cold tiles and distant, elder-orgy dissonance.

Lee-Lee trudged up the servant's stairs back to the second floor, almost exactly the way she used to as a child. The smells and creaks of the house hadn't changed a single bit. She recalled games of hide-and-seek with her brother Casey that usually ended with a family manhunt due to the ever-growing size of the house from year to year. It never struck her as odd, the way the house would expand and grow, but the property wouldn't. Same as the other homes in town. Make it lavish but keep it quaint. Like a lure. As she reached the second floor, Uncle Lucas greeted her with a repentant smile.

"Been a while, Lilly," Uncle Lucas smiled despite the massive inconvenience.

"I go by Lee-Lee these days," she shrugged.

"Oh, that's right! Casey couldn't pronounce Lilly, so he called you Lee-Lee. Funny how change and inspiration could come from anywhere—anyone—at any time. How *is* Casey?"

"He's … doing great. Look, I'm so sorry for this, Uncle Lucas," Lee-Lee shook her head.

Uncle Lucas watched her crimson hair shimmy over her undercut. During shows, she would spike it as high as her mousse would hold it, and that all depended on the humidity.

"We just had nowhere else to go, and you and Aunt Gretta have always been so good to me."

"We paid for you to go to Berklee and pursue your passion for music."

"Which I cannot thank you enough fo—"

"—And you've used that education to drive around in a pitiful van with a gaggle of malcontents, performing in sketchy bars and clubs, with songs called 'Moose Knuckle Mashup', 'Taco Duck', and 'Ironman Died for Our Sins'?"

"Well, I mean, he *did*—wait, how do you know about those?"

"Because I'm a Busketeer!" Uncle Lucas laughed. The wind was knocked completely out of Lee-Lee's sails. "I've downloaded all of your songs and play them when I want to irritate Gretta. You have some truly strange taste, but a few songs really have potential, like 'Last Dance in the Graveyard'. That showcases your appreciation for Bach."

"I'm working on a new song in that vein. I'm thinking of using a harpsichord and a hurdy gurdy—if

I can score one. I want it to be hauntingly painful and beautiful, but I'm having trouble pushing through the lyric writing."

"It'll happen when it needs to. I have faith in you, kiddo."

Uncle Lucas' smile made Lee-Lee feel like she was a little girl again, performing a song on the piano that she picked up by ear.

"In all seriousness, though, you and the band can stay the night, perhaps even the weekend—but do not leave the house or open any door or window. Once Halloween and All Saint's Day are over, you can have the run of the town."

"I don't understand that, though, Uncle Lucas," Lee-Lee said with legitimate confusion.

"Pacton has some … strange … traditions. Ones that require adherence to the rules. And those rules are as simple as I've said."

"Why not barricade the doors and nail the windows shut?"

"Everyone in attendance—your friends notwithstanding—are quite familiar with what needs to happen and not happen tonight, so there wasn't any need to."

"I'll make sure they behave," Lee-Lee said, the tiredness of the day's journey had set in, and she would very much like a shower. "Now go smash some sabretooth cougar cooch, you weirdo."

3

"Aren't you the least bit curious?" Bella asked Mia, who was rummaging through her duffle bag in frustration. "Babe!"

"*What*, goddamn it?" Mia snapped back with a groan.

"The town, the red candles, the … everything!" Bella paused, realizing the disdain in her girlfriend's voice.

"Hold up—what the hell is up with you suddenly? You've been acting like someone who isn't shacking up in a gorgeous, New England mansion—*for free*—with her bomb-ass, lava-hot lover girl. We just had delicious food, there's clean sheets on a queen-sized bed, and … I dunno … *me*? I *might* be a check in the positive column, *right*?"

Bella winced, feeling like she's said too much. Mia had the tendency to exert control whenever she could. A toxic trait for sure, but it came from a trauma-survival paradigm. She would never get into it, and the band respected that, despite the eggshells they were forced to regularly traverse. Mia sighed.

"I'm sorry, babe, seriously," Mia said softly as

she walked over to Bella and embraced her from behind. Bella leaned back for a kiss. "You know I'm—I've got my issues …"

"Issues?" Bella chuckled. "Mama, you've got subscriptions to issues!"

They kissed again and something from across the street caught Bella's attention.

"Look at those two!"

She jerked away from Mia and studied two figures in long cloaks moving towards the guru gathering. Both had large hoods draped over their heads, and their cloaks undulated despite there being no wind.

"Are they fucking floating?" Mia asked. "Looks like they're wading through water."

"Wanna keep watching?" Bella asked with a wink and a playful shoulder swivel.

"Actually, it's Halloween and I don't give a tinker's shit about any of it. What I'd rather focus on is how hot the shower water can get, and how much hotter we can make it."

Mia held out her hand which Bella took without hesitation.

"Or …" Bella smirked, tugging Mia to the queen-size bed. "Maybe we can get a little bit dirtier first?"

4

"Hey, *hey*! You made it!"

The self-proclaimed 'Guru of Humanity's Salvation' exclaimed to the group of sojourners gathered in the parlor.

They've paid a pretty penny to become a part of Bruce J. Dukehouse's *Traveling Lightsmith Movement*. Poorly regurgitated new age flatus with a folksy spin to make it more homespun and as common as a As Seen on TV endcap at Walmart. It was all fluff and bullshit, of course—hence the *traveling* part of the name. Once the gospel had been spread, the contributions deposited, Dukehouse and his core disciples would be in the wind. You could always buy their rancid patchouli health ointment and *totally legit* remote energy healings online, though.

"Through all of the obstacles you've faced, you are here—saying goodbye to your jobs, your familial relationships, your 401(k)s. You've told the world that you are tossing the shackles of oppression to the four winds and embracing your true calling! Serving me!"

"Serving *you*?" one of those gathered piped up.

"I mean in a spiritual way!" Dukehouse backpedaled. "Serve *with* me in this enlightenment evolution."

"And what do you mean, say goodbye to our jobs?" another participant called out. "I thought this was going to be a weekend thing. We meditate, take some drugs, and maybe hook up."

"We're here to create a community that will spiritually rise above all terrestrial matters. Together we will etch out a new global consciousness that will propel us into nirvana."

Dukehouse attempted to speak with authority. It *sort of* worked.

"Etched like a wood carving?" another in attendance asked. "Shouldn't we do something a little more … like, permanent?"

"Bro, haven't you seen the works of Albrecht Dürer?" yet another attendee chimed in.

"Hell, yes I have, bro! But Dürer engraved, not etched."

"Semantics …"

"Hey, HEY!" Dukehouse shouted. "Your focus is on *me* tonight! You came all this way to ascend to the next level. Why bicker on silly … uh … world … shit? Yes, there will be meditation. Yes, there might be drugs–unless one of you is a narc, then no there won't be—and hooking up, as one of you had mentioned, is entirely on the table so long as you give yourselves over to my lightsmithing. I'm here for you! Are *you* here for you? Matter of fact, let's refocus with a song. Cindy, would you get me my guitar?"

Dukehouse threw his left hand out and prodded his fingers like he was fork-porking an electrical outlet. A tired and sad-looking pixie of a woman in a dirty, white nightgown approached with a sticker-graffitied acoustic guitar and held it towards him lifelessly. After several minutes of tuning the beat-up instrument, he began to sing. His voice was an amalgamation of Jim Croce and Kermit the Frog.

"There's a light
Shining bright
Casting shadows from our souls.
Follow me and see
That this truth will set you free
Your stories are not yet told.

Give me everything (hey hey!)
So you'll have nothing.
And I'll give you nothing (hey hey!)
So you'll have everything.

Lightsmithing

Your savings aren't saving you
Toss them my way
Your wives aren't serving you
Let me teach them how

Even though I have a thin di—"

The doorbell rang, interrupting the guru's cringe-filled song. Dukehouse huffed as hard as he could but could not muster one shred of masculinity. He shot his acolyte, Cindy, another look, but she just shrugged. One of the attendants, a man named Denny, stood up and answered the door. He recoiled as he saw the two gaunt, shrouded faces of the visitors. Denny thought they looked like the wraiths or ghouls or whatever was chasing Viggo Mortensen and Tobey Maguire in that ring movie. Their iridescent eyes pierced the darkness of the hoods.

"Trick or treat," the taller ghoul said with a

voice that Denny couldn't pinpoint whether he heard it in his ears or his head.

"Bro, I appreciate the dedication to the costumes, but now's not the best time. The … teacher … or, like, shaman …" Denny turned to Dukehouse. "What *do* we call you, bro?"

"Lightsmith!" Dukehouse shouted. "I hammer the darkness from each of you until you are all luminous!"

The ghouls tittered under their hoods. The taller one sighed.

"Delightful, truly. We do so revere the delusional machinations of the human ego. Destined to dust, yet you cling to lies and fairytales to cope with your inescapable expiration. I cannot—and will not—blame you, however …"

The hood came down, revealing a face that *could* have been etched by Albrecht Dürer. A once handsome face now gaunt with sunken pools of ink where human eyes formerly rested. Two iridescent orbs shone preternaturally through the gloom. His bald head resembled marble.

"… for horrors have always beleaguered your kind."

There was a tremor among the congregation. Fear and confusion swept through the decadent bed and breakfast—even more so when the second ghoul removed her hood, allowing her pale-golden tresses to tumble free. Her eyes shimmered. Her smile, however, provoked terror.

"Her teeth are all fangs!" a member shrieked, causing the smile to grow.

"What should we do—ah—*Lightsmith*?" Denny turned to where his exalted teacher once stood. "Oh …"

"Your false prophet ran away mere moments

ago. But do not despair, for we bring *actual* salvation. You will suffer and toil no more!" The taller ghoul smiled with his own nightmare mouth.

Denny, having his fill of this disturbance, approached the taller ghoul and tried to usher him towards the door with a hand upon its chest.

"Alright, who-and-whatever the fuck you two are—your Halloween shenanigans are over. Time to go."

Denny could not budge the creature. He couldn't even make it sway.

"My name, peasant, is Cicero, Caesar's Scourge." The ancient vampire smiled and tilted its head in a mock greeting. "My companion is Embla, shieldmaiden of a long-forgotten tribe of Norse heathens."

Denny pushed harder.

"Your commitment to the gimmick is excellent, really, but you both have to leave now!"

"Yeah!" another member yelled. "If you're actual vampires, you gotta be invited in and shit! None of us invited you in, so you gotta go!"

"But we *were* invited …" Embla spoke with a voice like a harp in a cavern.

She pointed to the flickering red candle on the doorstep.

"Invitation is a paltry folkloric anecdote to create a sense of safety—but a pact is a pact."

Her voice hardly exhibited any traces of her Scandinavian origin save for a few words, but her shimmering eyes were as intense as they were when she was a part of a shield wall. Embla's body count had been in the double digits prior to becoming one of the undead. There was no use in keeping score since.

"Indeed," Cicero grinned devilishly. "Speaking of *pacts* … welcome to Pacton."

The vampire took Denny's hand and bit clear through the metacarpals, amputating every finger but the thumb. Before the screams could crescendo, Embla closed the door in a blur of speed, then pounced on the closest member. She sunk her gaping maw into their throat and tore it free in a slurry of fleshy strands and gushing blood.

Swirling and churning the meat in her mouth, Embla then spat the chunks to the wood floor and laughed with a mouth full of sharp, thorn-like fangs. These weren't the vampires of cinema, with their slender incisors and fragile romantics. These were the beasts of legend—of the cold, dark woods—whose savagery had been trauma-blocked over the centuries so folks would actually venture out of their homes. It's quite astonishing what humanity will normalize in order to feel safe and in control.

Limbs were strewn. Heads were smashed together like empty beer cans. The screams of would-be cultists were drowned out by the laughter and gratifying moans of the fiends. Try as they might, those still alive would attempt an escape, but were caught before they'd even touched a doorknob or windowpane. Their spines were then crushed, and they were tossed onto a pile with the rest of the shattered, quivering smorgasbord.

Cicero paused and drew the iron-heavy air through his nose with a deep breath. The electricity derived from the charnel buffet coursed through his every fiber. He recalled his days as a Roman commander, cleaving the enemy with his spatha—a straight long sword, much like a Viking's—with *Gloria Aut Mors* inscribed along the blade. He relished not only the sinking of the steel, but the wrenching free of it from hewn flesh.

There was only one battle Cicero ever lost—though he wouldn't recount it that way. It wasn't in the name of his Emperor, but in the name of ignorance. A beast in female form. The only female he couldn't overpower and take as his subjugate. Try as he might. Her name was Bauninshega of Sumaria, or to the biblical scholars, *Shinar*.

Cicero came across the ancient one during one of his campaigns to wrest even more earth for his soon-to-be-betrayed emperor. Cicero had difficulty remembering exactly where it took place, but he would never forget the image of the raven-haired crone standing in the shadow of a large hut adorned with the bones and skin of both beast and human—a garish mosaic of death and tribute. Cicero's troops had razed the village, slaughtered the occupants, raped and mutilated whom they could, yet that one structure remained unscathed. Cicero and his troops swarmed the hut and the shrouded, grinning crone.

"Step into the sunlight, dog!" Cicero commanded. The crone cackled. Her voice was the shattering of decorated kilned clay.

"Come and claim me, tiny Roman. Little conqueror …"

The crone's laugh was so hard it shook the bones upon her hut.

Cicero sneered, "I wouldn't waste the energy or the time for one so lowly as you, bitch."

With a gesture, one of his troops rushed in. Bauninshega receded like a shadow into the hut. The soldier followed. A scream pierced the air. That of a man. Followed by an alarming gurgle. Cicero pointed to three other soldiers then to the darkened hut. They obeyed and entered. Minutes passed without any sign of struggle. The crone emerged, still in the shade of the awning. Her smile was bloody and wide. Her skin was tighter and looked more like stained marble than before. *Surely a trick of the shadows,* Cicero thought. He ordered his archers to rain down upon the crone and her macabre hut. Every arrow ricochetted off their mark as if twigs in a strong gust. Bauninshega smiled and sunk back into the hut.

"More men *must* be the answer … send them to me without delay, child."

Her laugh was akin to a winter's chill, or an itch impossible to scratch.

"I am no child, *cunnus*!" Cicero roared. "Archers! Light this blight upon the asshole of creation ablaze!"

The archers dipped their arrows in the pitch pouches they carried for such occasions and fired at will. The arrows once again bounced and extinguished to the ground like clattering sticks. Bauninshega shook her head as if she were a teacher and her prized pupil had forgotten how to wipe their own ass.

"How many men are you prepared to sacrifice to me?" she asked.

"To purge your kind from the world and my sight?" Cicero barked. "As many as it takes!"

"Excellent," the crone grinned. "Prove it."

"No … I think not." Cicero paused upon reflection. "I know not what witchcraft you vex us with, but I know more kindling to douse a fire would be folly."

He motioned to his second in command, a resolute veteran named Adrian, who had stood side-by-side with Cicero since his seventh campaign into the dark heathen woods of the Northwest. He pulled him in close.

"Sir?"

"I will go alone. Take the remaining garrison to the far side of the village and wait for me to return."

"But Sir… her magic is quite formidable!"

"Jupiter himself once sanctified me in a vision, my ward." Cicero grinned and kissed Adrian's forehead. "What is this bitch to that of one with such a blessing?"

"I do not mean to question, Sir … but the others who have fallen by her hand?"

"They didn't have the dream I did."

"I-I—shall obey, Sir!" Adrian gripped his superior's hand quickly but firm, then followed orders perfectly befitting a general's right hand.

"Good lad, now off with you." Cicero turned back to the hut and drew his sword. "Crone! I would have a word with you!"

Bauninshega emerged from the nebulousness of her den and stretched out her left hand in a seductive beckoning. The fingers exposed to sunlight slowly began to smoke and smolder, causing the now youthful looking adversary to suck her teeth in what can only be described as excruciating ecstasy.

"Come now, conqueror, let us play together in the shadows …"

"Cicero?"

Embla placed her viscera-soaked hand upon her maker's shoulder. He held one of the last Lightsmith cultists aloft by the throat.

"If you're not going to eat that, I will."

"Hm? Oh!" Cicero snapped from his memory with an ethereal chuckle. "Apologies, my dear—I was a thousand years away. Allow me …"

The ancient ghoul sunk the fingers of his right hand into the cultist's pelvis and with his left and pulled her in half like a fortune cookie. Cicero handed Embla the lower half as the intestines slither-spiraled to the floor.

"Let us play together in the shadows," he said before crashing his nightmare maw into his victim's chest.

"A delightful phrase."

The Viking maiden smiled, then buried her face into the exposed slurry of bowels with heavy slurps. Once Embla had had her fill, she tossed the half-body aside, ripped the top half from her maker playfully, then threw it upward so the head lodged into the ceiling.

"Meat piñata!" she laughed.

Her dark humor had not abated despite her millennia of inhumanity. Cicero was often elated by the fact that her wit had, if anything, evolved with the times.

Cicero took a section of dangling intestine and twirled it like a lasso. "Yippie kai-ay!"

His chuckle was something not heard for many a dark year, and Embla was delighted. In her swoon, she embraced her maker and zealously licked the gore from his face.

"Take me, maker," she panted. "Or I shall take you!"

"My dark love …" Cicero whispered, "… our feast is not yet complete. Let us pack down our lust like gunpowder until our bellies are swollen, mouths flush, and our eyes ablaze with the souls of human cattle."

"You seem a better poet than our dear Cillian." Embla pulled away with a taunting scoff, referencing the missing third member of their party. "Now … where would this quivering quim of a holy man hide from us? Even now I sense his hummingbird heartbeat, his trembling breath, his piss-soaked pants. I don't even think he's worth feasting on."

"Seems you're quite the poet as well, you know," Cicero grinned and slid his hand from her shoulder to her breast, then down to her crimson left hand and gripped firmly. "Let us finish this scene so we may move our grisly narrative along and the dreaded rays of dawn cannot claim our folly."

"Then we fuck."

"Then we fuck."

The two vampiric ghouls embraced and touched tongues, sending a copper current of ecstasy throughout their bodies.

"Come … the hunt is still upon us."

They stalked up the stairs to the second floor and paused at a door adorned with an ornate sigil engraved with blood and silver. The myriad of twisted, barbed shapes was a promise. A pact. One that the vampires would uphold, so long as the rules were obeyed. Cicero knocked gently with a smile.

"Y-yes?" a timid voice answered promptly. "B-Benefactor?"

"We're having a *splendid* time, Mr. Kelly." Cicero said.

"Excellent! En-enjoy!" Mr. Kelly stammered. Cicero moved down the hallway to another room which did not have the sacred sigil embellishment. He looked to Embla who simply nodded, and he opened the door to a quaint New England-style bedroom with a seaside motif.

"I never did like the sea," Cicero stated. "Too vast. Too deep. Too many monsters, and nothing to eat!"

With a flick of his wrist, he sent the queen-sized bed flying to the wall, revealing a quivering, sniveling, would-be guru of enlightenment clutching his acoustic guitar in the fetal position.

"Well now, look at what we have here … a monster revealed."

"H-hey—hey! I think you—I think I'm more

useful alive!" Dukehouse stammered and clambered to his knees in supplication. "Or-or-or make me one of you!"

"Hm … another one of *us*?" Cicero rubbed his blood-soaked chin. "I haven't sired a new vampire since our beloved Cillian. Much to your chagrin, my darling. Should we consider turning this sniveling, wretched, fraction of a man into an apex predator?"

"You cannot be serious, Cicero," Embla clutched his robe and pulled him close.

Cicero simply smiled and winked—a telltale sign that her maker was playing with his food. She exhaled sharply in contempt but didn't ruin the ruse.

"Rise, snake oil salesman," Cicero said with his left hand aloft.

Dukehouse did as ordered and stood on piss-soaked feet and wobbly knees. The vampire placed his ancient hands upon the shoulders of the charlatan.

"You are to become … another meat piñata!"

Up Dukehouse went, his head lodging into the ceiling. His body twitched as the brain told the nerves that the game was up. The fraud factory was shutting down. The vampires laughed.

"May I?" Embla asked, holding the guitar like a baseball bat.

"No, love. I would relish the opportunity to practice *my* swing."

Cicero spoke sincerely, yet with the authority of a vampiric maker. She handed Cicero the instrument and he swung it with more force than he anticipated. The guru's lower half flew across the bedroom with intestine streamers and lodged into the far wall. Dukehouse's fingers still twitched wildly, indicating that pain was still active, which caused the old ghouls to smile.

"Now that the appetizer is over, let us check in

on Cillian and see how he's been getting on."

The two moved through the house like drunken lovers—stealing kisses here, fondling engorged/throbbing body parts there. Every cell in their bodies pulsated with human blood, and it was pure jubilation. They staggered to the front door and stepped into the crisp Autumn air.

5

"Well, that was definitely in our top-five-fucks," Bella said before a sharp exhale.

Mia's head rose and fell with each of Bella's breaths. Mia ran her fingers over her lover's soft, sweat-clammy flesh; cascading over breasts, across a Rubenesque belly, then back up to the collar bones, where her fingertips softly tickled Bella's neck. Mia's hand then caressed Bella's left arm. Slowly, methodically, trying to avoid the bramble of scars near the wrist. Her right arm was no different, and Mia knew to avoid those trauma spots, even though the avoidance was a potential argument tight roping between acceptance and shame. Love is a minefield at times.

"You smell like inexpensive bologna," Mia chuckled.

"Way to kill the moment, Lee Harvey Oswald." Bella playfully shoved her off in mock disdain.

"Unlike Oswald," Mia swung her legs over the side of the bed and scanned the room for her cigarette pack. "I *actually* did it."

"Fine, slayer of moods. I'll take a shower, then

we should check in with the others."

Bella lurched from the bed and stretched away her favorite aches.

"Why bother?" Mia asked while rummaging through the pile of crap on the floor for her cigarettes. "The boys are downstairs having an AARP-orgy, and I'm confident that Dax is trying his best to get back into Lee-Lee's pretentiously puckered butthole."

"Seriously," Bella chuckled as she paused at the bathroom threshold. "You should be the one writing our lyrics."

"You flatter me, bologna queen. Though, I also happen to agree."

Mia turned back to her scavenger hunt. Bella smiled and closed the door behind her. Mia pulled the pack of Mal Burros from her fanny pack and sighed in relief. Instinctively, she bit the butt of one and ripped it from the pack like a velociraptor would a tendon from a Jurassic Park visitor. Holding the lighter to the tip she thought, *shit, I can't light this without setting off a fire alarm*, so she shuffled to the window and unlocked it with shaky fingers. She noticed the two cloaked whackadoos across the street stopped walking at the sound of the latch's *clack*. She pushed the window open ever so slightly then placed the lighter to the cigarette and gave it a flick, causing it to flip from her hand to the floor. In a fluid motion she swooped down, snatched the lighter, then rose igniting it to the cherry red glow of the cigarette. As she exhaled, she saw a set of gruesome gaping grins against the glass.

The acid had long taken hold of Jessie's mind before he found himself balanced on a large ottoman, overlooking an undulating sea of vocally writhing geriatric flesh while working his accordion like the only bellows keeping the Earth's core glowing. But there he was, feverishly pumping and gesticulating on the buttons and keys like he'd finally found his purpose:

Orgy Oompah Music.

"Snap that coochie, Madge!" Jessie shouted.

Madge's head turned into Max Headroom's and smiled while she smashed harder down on her neighbor's unicorn horn of a dong.

"Stop screaming at the participants!" Rafael—also tripping proverbial balls—barked, pelvis-packed into Mrs. Joelsteen. "It's bad enough that you *insist* on playing your pervert pirate overtures, but no one here needs directions on debauchery! I don't *care* if you are half alpaca now—oh—" Rafael turned his attention back to his current task. "You're well past menopause, right?"

"Shut up and cream pie me, dipshit!" Mrs. Joelsteen ordered.

Her body turned into Hieronymus Bosch's triptych, *The Garden of Earthly Delights*, which took all control out of his hands. Rafael saw the subdermal colors erupt through his member and into Mrs. Joelsteen's nethers like a herd of technicolor zebra barracuda. His seed slithered through her torso, to her neck, then caressed her face like the children of a dying grandparent, finally erupting through her eyes like an epiphany of light and confetti.

"Eres la luz de mi alma, mujer de cebra blanca," Rafael cooed. His peripheral vision caught two darkened entities descending the main stairs holding Jack-o-lanterns with a glowing crimson radiance. As they approached, he realized that they weren't carved pumpkins but the severed heads of Mia and Bella, carried by grinning, blood-spattered goth Teletubbies.

"Wait … what the fuck?" he queried as he dislodged from Mrs. Joelsteen.

Embla was upon him before the mucus of intercourse had a chance to fully separate. She embedded her maw into Rafael's neck and pulled him to the ground like a lioness would a gazelle. Cicero—who looked to Jessie like a hurried five-year-old's crayon scribbled Dracula— threw Bella's head into the face of Jim Van Etten, Pacton's mayor who was right in the middle of receiving a rusty trombone from Meredith Bush, town planner and self-proclaimed elite local author. Electric hummingbirds exploded from the impact, spattering against the ceiling in a kamikaze of sparks. Cicero exhaled a black spiral of feathers then smiled.

"This brings me back to those dear old days of the Republic," he said thoughtfully, with a tinge of nostalgia, then pointed to Jessie. "Please continue your jaunty compositions, maestro."

Jessie played on, eyes wide and snake fingers trembling.

6

Lee-Lee's fingers hovered over the piano's keys like a healer searching for the place of sickness. She had put this off too long, she knew, but that's how humans sometimes cope with loss and suffering. Stuff it down until it becomes something far more formidable and damning. She debated using The Augmented 4th—also known as the chord of evil—but her composition was one of sadness, not the divine hatred toward an unjust god. She settled for a C minor chord and her intuition took over. At first her fingers struck the keys like an executioner's axe, then gradually softened to that of falling leaves on cold, frosted soil. She slowly inhaled and held it until her lungs and esophagus ached. Then she began.

"Rest your head, my love
Sleep and dream beneath electric constellations
moving lights and simple songs
crafted by indifferent hands
and yet …

Life gets so much harder when you've grown

But … you'll never get to know
and here we are
singing this lullaby lament

I just knew there'd be a song in your soul
lightning in your eyes
and thunder in your heart

But now
we'll never know

These plans we set in motion
lost now to the ocean
Drifting … sinking
those plans all fell apart

Like a dream
a hope gone by
a dull memory, a scent faded
a lamenting lullaby …"

"Lee?" Dax sheepishly entered the music room.

Lee-Lee took in a startled breath and steeled herself with the exhale.

"Sh-shit, I'm sorry for … well …"

"Just say your piece, Dax, and let me get back to it."

Lee-Lee wiped a tear from her eye with her right palm. Dax moved closer and attempted to place his left hand on her shoulder, but it only hovered then retracted with a curl of fingers. He wanted nothing more than to touch her, comfort her, be the rock she always praised him for being before … well, before.

"I'm sorry for interrupting, it's just that we haven't really, *truly* made time to talk about us and …

the thing."

"Don't call what happened *the thing*, okay? That's fucking insensitive." She turned her back on Dax, which sent a sharp pain straight through his chest.

"No, enough!" Dax said sternly while forcing himself onto the piano bench. Facing the music room, Dax looked at the many instruments hanging on the lacquered wooden walls and wished to have the same one day. He rubbed his chest and cleared his throat.

"Not trying to detract from the pain you feel, but you aren't the only one who lost a daughter that day, okay?"

"I … that's …"

Dax's words struck Lee-Lee hard. Her left hand sprinted atop the piano keys swiftly as one would the Rosary, trying to find focus.

"What happened wasn't your fault. Not even a little. You did *everything* right."

"Wasn't yours either," Lee-Lee sniffled. She was slightly startled by Dax sobbing at her admission. The two embraced.

"All I've ever wanted to hear, babe," Dax pulled away and wiped his face on his shirt. "Felt like you had it in your head that I was the one who cause it … but I wanted nothing more than to—" he bawled into his hands, "—be a dad."

Lee-Lee kissed the back of his right hand. He then wrapped that arm around her and slowly pulled her to the floor with him as he slid from the bench. Dax's shirt became drenched by the combination of their tears. Neither cared.

"Less than five percent," Lee-Lee whispered.

"What's less than five percent?"

"Second-trimester miscarriage odds …"

"*Fuck*," Dax shook his head.

"Probably microplastics and 5G-radio-tower-testicular Covid transmitted by robot birds. You do know that birds aren't real, right?" Lee-Lee declared, causing Dax to sputter.

"You're too much, babe," he chuckled before pressing his lips to hers, who this time, leaned in deep for it.

"Better than not being enough, right?"

They kissed again; tears and snot be damned.

"That song you were singing … that about Lorelei?" Dax asked. Lee-Lee squeezed his hand tight.

"Y-yeah," she said softly, unaccustomed to hearing her daughter's name aloud.

"It's heartbreakingly beautiful, Lee. What's it called?"

"'Lullaby Lament'," she said, then cleared her throat to shake the melancholy from her vocal cords.

"Damn, that's good! I don't think anyone should be on the track but you."

Their attention turned to the rising screams from the main floor. Apparently, the orgy was hitting a unified crescendo.

"I wouldn't mind your input, honestly," Lee-Lee smiled. "Maybe we can heal through this together. I'm sorry if I—holy shit, do you hear those old whackos down there? I can't tell if they're having the time of or end of their lives."

As if on cue, Uncle Lucas smashed into the room, covered in sweat and blood. His no-longer-white robe hung heavy with gore.

"Come with me!" Lucas screamed. "Now!" He ushered them to the door towards the back of the room that opened to a small spiral staircase which led up to the third floor. The spiral was so tight that Dax had difficulty contouring his frame as he ascended.

"The fuck is going on?" Lee-Lee groaned as she banged her elbow on the metal column. Uncle

Lucas looked back at her with a fear in his eyes that she had never seen in another human being.

"Just follow! If we get to the saferoom I'll tell you everything."

"Why the hell does your uncle have a saferoom?" Dax barked. Claustrophobia, compounded with road-weariness, and this new unseen threat was causing him to panic. "Rich white people, I swear!"

Uncle Lucas opened the door to the third-floor hallway and waved the two up quickly. Lee-Lee saw her aunt in a doorway a dozen yards away gesturing frantically.

"It's quiet now! Hurry before they come!" Aunt Gretta cried, referring to the downstairs decibel drop.

All three ran the short-yet-seemingly-vast distance to the saferoom door. Uncle Lucas practically shoved Lee-Lee inside, then froze as Dax paused and peered down the hallway to the main staircase where a diminutive, trembling shadow stood, emitting traumatized notes from an accordion.

"Jessie!" Dax shouted.

Uncle Lucas grabbed his arm and attempted in vain to pull him into the room.

"Come on, Dax! We have seconds!" Uncle Lucas yelled.

Dax shrugged Uncle Lucas' hand off.

"I'm not leaving anyone behind!" Dax shouted, running as fast as he could towards his bandmate.

The breath from Lee-Lee's lungs vanished instantly at the sight of her one great love sprinting towards uncertain doom. Behind Jessie a shroud began to form from the main staircase.

"Get back here now!" Uncle Lucas bellowed as the stairwell shroud focused like a blurry camera aperture into the solid forms of Cicero and Embla.

Dax scooped Jessie—accordion and all—up in a fireman's carry and ran like hell. Cicero smiled at such easy prey and turned to his Viking bride who seemed a touch out-of-sorts.

"Embla, if you please … ?"

He looked curiously as his beloved as she stared at her fingers with the wonder of a child seeing fireworks for the first time.

"Darling? Our prey?"

"My hands are made of light, my love!" Embla exclaimed, wiggling her fingers. "Do you see the light? I haven't seen a glow so brilliant since my last morning as a mortal. You …" she looked upon her maker and gasped. "Your skin …" she whispered as she caressed Cicero's face. "Like marble … shimmering and flush with thousands of tiny blood-lit veins! Do you hear the chorus? There is a man singing through a bullhorn with a choir behind him. It is garish but beautiful in its way."

"What in the seven hells has happened to you, my love?"

Cicero took her by the arms and gave her a firm shake. She laughed at the neon butterflies that escaped her mouth.

"I think one of those fuck pigs had drugs in their system." Embla chuckled.

Cicero sneered as he heard the bedroom door lock down the hall. He rushed to it and railed against the sigil-protected wood.

"Lucas!" Cicero roared. "What has befallen my love?"

"How the fuck should I know?" Lucas shouted back with terror in his voice. "Why are you even here in my home? We weren't a tithe house this year!"

"And yet, with the simple opening of a window, you have violated the pact and have *become* one." Cicero ran his finger over the sigil that was the sole thing that kept him from the flock.

"Fuck." Uncle Lucas uttered, glaring at his young guests with more anger than he anticipated. "Lily. One of your people ruined everything. I warned you, didn't I?"

"You don't know that!" Lee-Lee countered with a furrowed brow.

"You should never have come here!" Aunt Gretta shook her head vigorously. "We never should have answered the door."

"But you did!" Dax stated, looking for something to barricade the door with.

"Yeah, you can't un-ring that bell, Aunt Gretta. Sorry." Lee-Lee threw her hands up in defeat. "But here we are. Sorry that your orgy got fucked!"

"Lee—" Uncle Lucas remonstrated her lack of tact. Aunt Gretta had just about lost her shit.

"This was a celebration! Those people were the only decent goddamn people left in Pacton! And your idiot friends got them killed because they couldn't follow simple, fucking instructions!"

"You don't know that!" Dax enhanced tension.

"Acid …" Jessie added. "And yes, it was our fault. Papa Smurf is telling me that I should have been a middle school teacher."

"What are you talking about, Jess?" asked Lee-Lee.

Jessie stared at the door while Papa Smurf shook his head in disappointment.

"Me and Boom-Boom took a few acid tabs before hitting the orgy—great orgy, by the way, sir," Jessie said, saluting Uncle Lucas. "Seriously, this town is flush with quality vintage poon and peen."

"Get to the goddamn point, idiot!" Aunt Gretta yelled. Each word swirled from her mouth like a series of drunken dragonflies.

"The two whatevers on the other side of that door came down with Bella's and Mia's heads. Then, the Hitler hottie chomped on our boy," Jessie stammered, calmer than one who has witnessed such atrocities should have been.

"Lucas and Gretta Allore!" Cicero called from the hallway. "We apologize for ruining your bacchanal, but the pact had been broken. A window on the second floor, I'm afraid. She was sweaty with sex and tasted succulent. But rules are rules. I ask you now, what is affecting my beloved Embla?"

"Two of the idiots took acid before joining the … bacchanal," Aunt Gretta groaned.

"It was a gore-gy!" Jessie yowled and hit three sour notes on his accordion.

"Who is that?" Cicero asked.

"The *second* idiot," said Aunt Gretta.

"Send him out and we will spare the rest. I would like to know what his tainted blood would do to me."

"Well, that's fair." Jessie stated and walked towards the door.

"Agreed," Aunt Gretta nodded.

Dax piloted Jessie from the door as Lee-Lee chastised her aunt.

"You can't fucking be serious! I will knock you the *fuck* out before I let you feed my friend to those things!"

"One life for four, Lilly," Aunt Gretta said coldly. "I know you were never good at math, but—"

"—We're *not* opening that door," Uncle Lucas interjected. "We open the door, and we break the second pact."

"Rules are rules," Dax added. "Creepy motherfucker said as much."

"Exceptions can be made, Lucas Allore,"

Cicero stated.

Uncle Lucas considered those words heavily but ultimately knew in his heart that the nocturnal nightmares should not be trusted at their word.

"A pact is a pact, Lord Cicero," Uncle Lucas said into the door. "Derivations without proper ceremony are dubious and not to be trusted. My sincerest apologies … Lord."

"Apologies are suppositories for peasants, Allore!"

Cicero crashed his fist onto the door. The entire room shook yet remained intact. The sigil held true. "I do not know why I am bothering to address cattle. Perhaps it is that my innards are supplicated by the bounty this town has yet again provided. But you, dear Lucas, have disappointed me."

"I want to see the sky, beloved!" Embla wailed. She attempted to pull Cicero from the door, but he stood fast despite her incredible strength.

"You have until we return to make your decision—one life for the rest. Otherwise, I will make a few—addendums—to our pact."

With that ultimatum, Cicero allowed Embla to pry him from his diabolical diplomacy. Uncle Lucas quickly moved to the opposite wall of the large room, and tapped a key on a tablet, bringing a dozen wall-mounted monitors to life. The group anxiously watched the ghouls dance down the stairs, through the ghastly landscape of the main floor, then out the front door.

"Uncle Lucas," Lee-Lee began, unable to stop her hands from trembling. "Please, tell us what the fuck is happening. You at *least* owe us that."

"Sure, kid, but first I'd like to get dressed."

7

"Pacton was incorporated in 1761," Uncle Lucas said over his shoulder as he buttoned his pants.

His eyes darted towards the security monitors in case the vampires returned, but fortunately, the screens still only displayed the mutilated corpses of his guests.

"Honey, what are you doing?" he asked his wife who stood motionless and staring into the open wardrobe. He caressed her shoulders, causing her to shudder. "Gretta, what's going on?" She turned to him with a vacancy in her eyes.

"I … don't see the point in getting dressed …" she said. "... if we're all just going to die."

"You don't know that." Uncle Lucas kissed her forehead. "I'll radio Harris and then we can take the escape route."

"You guys have a way out of town?" Dax asked with optimistic shock.

"Not exactly, no. There's a secret stairway behind this wardrobe that leads to our basement. There, we go into the sewer, then make our way to the police station. From there, we either hunker down or maybe Chief Harris has an idea how to get out of town."

"Is it safe, that route?" asked Lee-Lee.

"No," Uncle Lucas replied. "There's nothing between this room and the police station that's protected by the sigil."

"Then we stay here," Dax suggested, noticing that this room was just as luxurious as the rest, with a king-size bed, lounge area, wall-mounted entertainment center, and what looked to be a bathroom bigger than any apartment he's lived in. "We wait it out until sunrise and then bug the fuck out."

"Hate to break it to you, young man," Uncle Lucas said as he pointed to the atomic clock hanging near the door, which read 9:45 p.m. "We're on the wrong side of midnight. Cicero and the others will make good on their demands long before the sun rises."

"Who the fuck is that guy anyway?" Dax asked.

"And you said *others*?" added Lee-Lee. "I saw the other with him, but there are more than that?"

"One more … hold on …"

Uncle Lucas opened a curio that contained trinkets and personal items that seemed too random to be a sensible collection. He pulled a ham radio out from the bottom shelf, set it on the dresser, then plugged it in. With a sharp click and static warble, he brought the machine to life.

"Chief Harris, come in," Uncle Lucas said into the microphone.

"That mic looks like one of those vagina vibrators," Jessie stated, able to see the frequencies fluttering from the machine like a flock of electric moths. "Wank Wand!"

"Sam, it's Lucas, please respond."

"How do you know he's got his—whatever

that is—on?" Dax asked, watching Aunt Gretta get dressed from the corner of his eye.

He had no idea how old she was, but goddamn, she was *stacked*, he thought.

"Every third Halloween, he has it on," Aunt Gretta stated. "Just in case."

"In case of *what*?" Lee-Lee shouted. "In case some fucking goddamn freaks come and rip people to shreds?"

"In case something goes wrong with the plan," Uncle Lucas furrowed his brow and tried again. "Chief Harris, come in. Do you read me?"

"There are no windows in this room," Jessie said to himself.

Suddenly, a sharp frequency crackle erupted from the radio. A static-dappled voice came through.

"Go for Harris."

"Sam, it's Lucas—we're in trouble."

"What happened, Lucas? You and Gretta alright? Sorry for the delay, I was explaining some things to our … guest."

"We're compromised, Sam—" Uncle Lucas rubbed his mouth then the sweat from his brow. "Someone opened something. I heard it was a window, but that's irrelevant. Van Etten is dead, his wife—hell, just about all the allies are gone. We need extraction. We need to follow the route."

"That's going to be tricky, Lucas. I suppose if you and Gretta are quiet enough you can make it here. And I've been working on a few things that might help. But that's *once* you two get here …"

"There's five of us," Uncle Lucas stated. "My niece and her friends are with us."

"That … complicates things," Chief Harris replied.

The hiss of frequency static emphasized the

pause between his thoughts.

"I'll tell you what—let me get the drone up and I'll scout where the bastards are and let you know when it's safe to move. The CCTV cameras just haven't been much help."

"How's he going to get the drone outside without opening a window or some shit?" Dax asked.

"He put it on the roof before sundown, as is part of the plan."

Uncle Lucas turned back to the receiver.

"Ok, Sam. Let us know. But please be quick."

"Quick as I can. Stand by." Chief Harris signed off, leaving the saferoom full of white noise.

"Alright, let's get some nourishment from the fridge, hydrate, and wait for the go-ahead." Uncle Lucas set the receiver back onto the dresser.

"Fridge? There's a fridge?" Jessie asked while trying to spot it.

Aunt Gretta moved to the tall mirror on the wall next to the entertainment center. She pressed her hand to it, causing it to become transparent, showing the contents inside.

"Why not hunker-down in style?" she said, then opened the door.

"Pimp my bunker," Dax chuckled, genuinely surprised that he could find levity in such a situation.

He took an apple and bottle of water. Jessie took a bottle of water as well, but nothing else. Lee-Lee shook her head and sat on the bed.

"I can't after what we just saw."

"At least hydrate," Aunt Gretta suggested.

Lee-Lee nodded in compliance and Dax walked a bottle over to her then plopped down beside her. Lee-Lee smiled softly and rested her head on his left shoulder.

"Ok, Uncle—" Lee-Lee began, then took a

swig of water. "While we wait for the go ahead, you might as well continue explaining why this town is so fucked up. Eighteen something-something?"

"1761," Uncle Lucas corrected.

His eyes returned to the screens for a moment, then he turned his attention back to the group.

"That's when the first settlers came. It wasn't easy making a life in this territory. Sure, there was logging and fishing, and hunting, but scarce else.

Bartholomew Hunkins—an entrepreneur of sorts—came to town a few years later with a chest full of riches he had earned from his various grifts and embezzlements. He saw this lakefront settlement as a destination spot for weary travelers looking to rest their head between here and there. He built a tavern and named it Come Inn. The town had an inn before it even had a name."

"That's pretty clever," Jessie said. The effects of the acid were starting to subside a little due to adrenalin, hydration, and straight exhaustion.

"Vampiric lore and all that. You have a place people come that has 'you're invited in to eat us' written right on the door."

He walked over to the trinket curio and picked up a stuffed panda bear. As he rubbed it with his thumb, he saw smatterings of floating red snowflakes coming from its fur. He quickly set it down and noticed that each item on display had an aura. He didn't dare touch another. Instead, he closed the curio doors and wiped his hands on his shirt. The psychic residue remained like psychedelic tie-dye.

"You're quite right, young man. There was something very bizarre about Bart Hunkins."

"Besides the unfortunate name?" Dax smirked. Lee-Lee elbowed his arm.

"He wasn't a typical colonial," Uncle Lucas

continued. “His accent was difficult to place, and his currency was from all over. He was a herald of The Benefactors, driven to make the town something grand. A place that would make a fortune from other’s misfortune. He told the townsfolk that he had a vision that would not only spare them a wretched death but make them rich beyond their imagination.”

“The Benefactors?” Dax asked. “Weak-ass name for a cadre of blood sucking fuck-knuckles, you ask me.”

“Cicero and Embla—the two whom you’ve had the displeasure of meeting already—and another female, Ming Yue, came to town mere months after the inn was fully operational. They came with riches beyond what anyone here had ever seen.

Life was difficult back then. The soil was rife with granite, making agriculture quite tricky. The townsfolk were trying their best to eke by with fishing and logging when they were promised wealth and prosperity in exchange for compliance. The Benefactors proposed that every three years, they would return and feast on whomever occupied the inn. The townsfolk would not speak of the horrors they would hear–or get involved in any way–and they would be paid handsomely. The vampires chose Samhain, I assume as a middle finger to All Saints’ Day. While other colonies prepared feasts honoring the saints, Pactonites prepared massacres. ‘Us or them’ was the unofficial town slogan.

Before even the second visitation came around, Hunkins had proposed to the town that they use their money to cultivate the area and properties and create a haven of sorts, for travelers and the like. Why settle for one inn when you can have many? With the promise of more money and affluence, the town agreed to sell their souls, so to speak. Hunkins had with him a contract and a sigil. The heads of households signed the contract in their blood and were given the sigil design to place wherever they didn't want the vampires to go. It was a pact."

"Pacton," Lee-Lee said. "The town finally had a name."

"Yes, and a dark, dark secret," Aunt Gretta added. She looked miserable in her slacks, purple blouse, and white running shoes. She had put together—she thought—an outfit that might best suit her needs in this situation. "One that we've kept for too fucking long."

"Agreed, my love." Uncle Lucas held his wife and kissed her deeply.

"Then, what is all this?" Lee-Lee asked. She plucked the half-eaten apple from Dax's hand and chomped on it. "The candles, and windows and whatever?"

"As time went on, it became harder to keep the truth from getting out. The town prospered in our vampire buffet until the early 1980s."

"That's what we should have named the band, by the way … *Vampire Buffet*."

Jessie stared at the security monitors and couldn't help but see the tormented ghosts of the dead mourning their violent ruin.

"*Fuuuuuuck*, this is some primo acid," he whispered.

"DNA and forensic investigation, surveillance, and communication had gotten advanced enough that it was only a matter of time before someone missed their relative who somehow vanished on their trip to the lakes region and hired someone with connections. But by then we were so rich that we—and I say we, but I mean the heads of town—hired a company to handle the cleanup."

"There's a company that gets rid of everything?" Dax asked. "This is some twisted shit. It was already twisted shit, but now it's Moebius Strip twisted shit."

"A Moebius Strip isn't that twisted, Dax," Jessie said.

"Sucker, it may not look it, but good luck getting out of it."

"Maybe more of a Gordian Knot," Lee-Lee offered. "But this is irrelevant. What was this company?"

"*Is*, really," Uncle Lucas said with a twinge of shame. "Tabula Rasa is the name, and their contract is still active to this day. In fact, they're scheduled to arrive around eight-thirty tomorrow morning."

"How could anyone make *anyone* disappear, let alone a whole town full of bodies?" Lee-Lee asked.

The understanding that her family members were not good people began to set in.

"We don't ask—they don't tell. Been that way for decades."

Uncle Lucas drank the rest of his water bottle then set it on the dresser next to the still-crackling radio.

"How could you do this? How could *any* of you do this?" Lee-Lee asked, feeling betrayed and disgusted.

Uncle Lucas let out a long, slow breath.

"We were all born into this, Lilly," he began, using the dresser to keep balanced. "We all had the best life could offer. Each generation born into this town knew nothing but wealth and all the benefits that brings. Your grandfather was born into it, your mother … nearly you. You were supposed to be my successor. Either Gretta or—myself—are unable to create life, so every-thing pointed to you. But we didn't—your mother didn't—want you to have anything to do with this nightmare, so she left. Gretta and I understood. Truth be told we were sick of the pact. We wanted out, as did many others in town. Most of us have sustained our fortunes through investments and the like; we didn't need blood money."

"Any *more* blood money, you mean," Dax added.

"Hey, it's not like we could—" Aunt Gretta interjected but was cut off by Uncle Lucas' raised hand.

"Things aren't so cut-and-dry, kid. When you're born into this, you aren't shown a way out. No escape plan. Just follow tradition and enjoy your life. Keep the pact. Always. Besides every third Halloween, Pacton is a bustling postcard-perfect destination. When the time came, the council would choose which homes would be tithe houses, and the rest of us lock up and keep our heads down. But there are a bunch of us that have decided that the time has come to end this nightmare."

"Where are the so-called *rest of us*?" Lee-Lee asked, kind of already knowing the answer.

Uncle Lucas pointed to the monitors.

"Shit," Dax sighed. "We're on our own?"

"Not entirely," Uncle Lucas assured his young guest. "The chief of police is part of the plan, as are a few other houses—but we'd only just begun preparations, agreements. Hence the …"

"Orgy," Lee-Lee frowned. "You were having a celebratory bang sesh and we screwed it all up."

"That's actually spot on," Aunt Gretta nodded and downed a quarter of a bottle of Riesling in a series of gulps. "We had things set up so that in three years' time we would have purged this town of its perpetual evil."

"Well, in theory anyway."

Uncle Lucas took the bottle from his wife's hand and chugged down a sizable portion before giving it back. He wiped his mouth on his sleeve and looked again at the monitors.

"We're dealing with an ancient malevolence. I mean, who knows if any of the plans we made would work?"

"*Ancient Malevolence* is also a better band name than the one we have," Jessie said. He picked his accordion up and sighed. "If we survive this, I'd say your uncle should write our lyrics."

"We don't *have* a band anymore, Jess!" Dax shouted. "It's just us!"

The reality of the situation began to pierce the blanket of shock that enveloped the group. "F-fuck, man—we might die tonight!"

"Hey—hey, big guy." Jessie cradled Dax's face in his hands. To Jessie, Dax looked like a marble statue of an African god come to life. "You're black and still alive in a horror movie. You have already defied the odds of modern cinema. By modern cinema, I mean anything made prior to Jordan Peele's work. Or Tyler Perry's. Or—"

Dax placed a supportive hand on his bandmate's shoulder.

"You can stop, Jess. Thanks for that unique reassurance."

"You're a marble god," Jessie whispered as though every conversation should end that way. Maybe they should.

"Should we check on Chief Harris, love?" Aunt Gretta asked after diminishing another large quantity of wine. "I don't want to die here, but I absolutely do not want to die in the fucking sewer."

"It's only been minutes, but fine."

Uncle Lucas shook his head then pressed the

button on the receiver.

"Sam—Chief Harris, come in. Any update? Copy."

Three minutes passed until he tried again.

"Come in, Chief. Is it safe to move?"

An unfamiliar voice responded, deep and sandy. A voice one could easily hear in a commercial about a truck or erectile dysfunction medicine.

"Copy, uh, yeah. We are a-copying. Go for Chief Harris."

"Who are—oh, you're the reporter?" Uncle Lucas asked.

"Affirmative."

"You guys invited a reporter?" Lee-Lee asked but was shut down by her uncle's raised hand.

"Where is Chief Harris? Has he found anything?"

"He says the monsters have bypassed the party at the Goreman house and are standing in front of the Cobbler's place. Doing nothing. Over."

"Good a time to move as any, right?" Dax said.

"Should we move then?" Uncle Lucas asked.

"Stand by … over. Sam says no. Too risky. He's got the drone way up high so they don't notice, but he says he's sure they'd notice you."

"That's nearly across town," Uncle Lucas stated.

"Over."

"What?"

"Sorry, I thought I needed to say over. I didn't say it. Over."

"Better now, over?"

"Yeah, thanks. Over."

"So, what do we do?" Uncle Lucas' irritation was rising with each transmission.

"Stay the fuck put until I contact you, Lucas!"

Chief Harris shouted in the background.

"Over," the reporter uttered.

Uncle Lucas groaned and dropped the receiver in frustration.

"Who are the Cobblers?" Lee-Lee asked.

Uncle Lucas snatched the bottle of wine from his wife's hand and took a few gulps.

"First-generation Pactonites," he said as he handed the bottle back. "And a rather tragic part of the plan."

8

Jim Cobbler blew out another candle. The remaining light danced across the features of his beloved wife of 45 years, Laura, and the vampire called Cillian. He was much younger than his cohorts, and less gruesome, though not by much. Black hair about cheek's length played across his vibrant green eyes.

As he sat in a wood-and-white-leather chair built in the 1930s, he smiled at his hosts who sat on a loveseat made of the same material on the opposite side of a modest mahogany coffee table. The sitting room was quaint despite the obvious notes of luxurious swank. Two cups of tea sat on the table. One was empty, the other full and quite cold.

"What's this we're doing then, Mr. Cobbler?" Cillian asked.

His Irish lilt was still noticeable despite his being undead since 1917.

He had fought in the short-lived Easter Rising, then became friends with W.B. Yeats and Ezra Pound. They said his poetry was too mundane to fully convey the emotion behind it. They lauded his potential while simultaneously condemning it.

Despite his love for poetry, it just wasn't his medium, and it tormented him to no end. He met Cicero and Embla on his way north, escaping the first world war.

Cicero loved how passionately Cillian spoke of his kinsmen and the verdant hills from which he hailed. Embla despised his cowardice, yet enjoyed his sense of humor, how easily he wept, and his impressive member. They played with him for months before offering him immortality.

Would he live forever? Could he? Should he? Cillian decided that death was inevitable regardless how long one could postpone it, so he agreed. The diabolical duo had become a terror throuple. Together they prowled battlefields and brothels alike, supping from the unfortunate, the destitute, and the dying.

"Please, call me Jim," the host said nervously as he lifted the teacup to his mouth.

"There's no steam from the cup, Jim," Cillian stated, cocking his head like a curious dog. "A proper cuppa is essential to longevity."

"Well, that's exactly just the thing … sir."

Jim didn't want to say that his hesitation was due to the lethal dose of cyanide swirling around his Lady Grey tea like a tiger shark at a shipwreck.

"*Sir*? No, thank you. Sir was the illegitimate title my father, Thomas O'Connell, gave himself, who was little more than a hooer and a drunkard. You can keep your *sir*, sir."

"I-I meant no disrespect …" Jim downed the bitter-cold drink in several nervous gulps. "I—*ah*—just don't know how to address you. We've known you and the others for so long, yet we've hardly interacted. I-I just don't want to offend."

"I'm dying," Laura stated weakly. "Brain … tum … ber."

"You want me t'change her?" Cillian asked, leaning back in the chair and crossing his right leg over the left.

"No …" Laura replied "… want to know … end like all the poor souls we've sent to … grave … together."

"I don't understand," Cillian said with a pang of sadness.

"When Laura found out about her … tumor, she found Jesus."

"—Who probably gave her the fekkin' thing to begin with," Cillian sneered.

"Either way, she wants to atone. Find a way to truly seek forgiveness. That's where she thought of you all."

"She's dying on the very night we're set to arrive? That's a bit convenient, don't yeh think?"

"Not at all," Laura said, slumping into the loveseat. "I … held … out …"

"It's poetic, really," Jim said before erupting in a score of retching coughs.

"How so?" Cillian asked with the sting and allure of that word in his mind: *Poetry*.

"A husband and wife," Jim began after wiping his mouth with a napkin. "And their family, causing so many deaths … so many losses … only to succumb to the weakness of the human body. The wife, wanting to suffer the same fate as her victims as a sort of penance, and her love-foolish husband not wanting to miss her for a minute, follows her."

"I think that's what I've been missing," Cillian held back tears of his own. "True love. I have had passions and pain, but they were all fleeting. Nothing truly matters unless it will vanish one undetermined day."

"Tha …" Laura said weakly, "… was p-poetry."

She was fading fast. Jim let out a startled cry which jarred Cillian. Finally, poetry. Death is a right bastard of inspiration.

"But I could *heal* you!" Cillian pled.

"Thank you," Jim said, then hacked again. "But we are this year's tribute. We don't have any children, so our nephew, William, will inherit the house and the pact."

Jim lied and hoped it wasn't perceivable.

"Fuck!" Cillian exclaimed despite himself. "In all my years I have never been able to express that kind of dedication even though I *knew* it coursed through my veins. I will do as you ask. For love. For poetry. Please, embrace for one last time."

"Thank you, my love." Jim cried and kissed his bride. "I'm sorry to have taken you down this path."

"No …" Laura whispered. "No sorry … only love."

Her eyes drifted, and Cillian moved with a panther's grace, taking Laura into his arms and sinking his fangs into her carotid artery. Her slow-pulsing blood plodded into the vampire's mouth. It tasted peculiar, but Cillian drank on. Laura's life slipped away as her hand did from her husband's. Cillian pulled from her neck with a gasp and set her back onto the loveseat.

"She is free." He fell back into the chair as though he had just performed a miracle.

"Please let me follow," Jim requested. Cillian shook his head.

"You're still so young, James," the vampire said, pressing the fingertips on both hands together like a steeple. "There is still time for you to find a new muse."

"No!" Jim jumped from the loveseat and tossed the coffee table aside in a panic.

He had to choose his next words carefully. His physical reaction may have jeopardized his and Laura's portion of the plan. But if there's anything the town had learned about Cillian the Vampire, it was that theatrics were considered currency. Jim could already feel the burning in his stomach. The next step is warmth in the veins, then the rapid decay of organs. Timing is everything.

"You call yourself a poet? You may have known countless loves in your time, but I've only known and needed *this* one! My Laura! I want to hold her hand before she steps in front of Saint Peter or the Hounds of Hell. Rejoice or burn together—that was our vow in this. Our … pact. Rapture or ruin. Please don't steal this from us. I beg you!"

As the warmth coursed through his body, the vampire stifled tears.

"Very well, James," Cillian rose then staggered slightly. "I cannot deny such a thing as … *hm* … that." The vampire's guts churned. His eyes began to burn. "What have you done?" He roared, sending crimson sputum across Jim's face.

"Wh-when was the last time you d-drank?" Jim stuttered, knowing that his death was drawing near—and not the way he was hoping. "S-sometimes when humans don't eat f-for a while they-they get queasy."

Cillian growled and lifted Jim off his feet by his throat.

"You. Manky. *Twat*!" Cillian shouted, releasing another volley of blood spatter. "You think I'm a bloody gobshite, do yeh?"

The cramping in his innards caused him to buckle and release Jim. Sadly, Jim didn't have much left in him to take advantage of it.

"Cillian, my darling!" Cicero called from the street. "Finish your devil's deed and join us."

Almost immediately, Cillian lurched through the doorway with his left hand on the back of Jim's neck. They both looked terrible.

"The shit is this?" Embla asked with a cocked head.

"I believe I have been poisoned," Cillian groaned, then puked red and black bile onto the pavement.

Cicero easily yanked Jim from Cillian's hand and gave him a sniff. He recoiled as one would when smelling rancid milk.

"He *is* contaminated; you fool! How did you not smell it?"

"The candles, Lord," Cillian admitted. "That must be it."

Embla tore Jim from Cicero's grip and threw him like a roll of toilet paper onto the roof. Jim's neck and lumbar snapped like a Styrofoam cup from the impact.

As the body tumbled to the immaculate lawn, the former shield maiden snarled. "Your poetry is the fog that obscures your thoughts and always brings you so close to ruin."

Cillian chuckled, as black froth seeped from his lips. "That … was … poetry."

"There is one more tribute house," Cicero stated, trying to conceal his concern. "We'll fill this fool with decent blood and set him right. I was imprudent to let him take a house on his own."

"This entire evening has been … odd," Embla said to no one in particular.

She wiggled her fingers and watched the electric rainbows shimmer forth.

"What's with the—*gurgle*—Viking?" Cillian

attempted a smile, but it was covered in blackened bile.

"She also drank from contaminated cattle. But her's was more of a psychedelic nature, not a toxic one. Enough chatter. The night grows thin, and we have so much more to desecrate."

"A moment, love." Embla plodded to the crumpled body of Jim Cobbler and lifted him as one would a discarded candy bar wrapper.

She plucked the red candle from its waxen cradle and brought the two into the colonial-style house. She placed Jim's battered corpse next to Laura's on the loveseat and stared thoughtfully for a moment at the two. She set the candle down and positioned the couple as though they simply fell asleep in each other's embrace. She watched their atoms dance and swirl above the bodies.

Souls perhaps? Embla mused.

She had difficulty remembering the last time she felt so mystical, though that word felt silly to her.

Once, Arne Erikson had given her a mushroom much like the berserkers took before battle. But this one enhanced the *senses*, not bloodlust. With it, she could feel every blade of Autumn grass caress her bare back. She could hear every creak of the Alder trees revealing to her their ancient secrets. She could see a parliament of grey owls on the boughs above, silently judging.

The sex was mediocre.

Embla pulled herself from her reminiscent reverie. She briefly, uncharacteristically, mourned her past life and how she would never enter Valhalla, or at the very least see her family should death ever claim her. *So be it,* she thought. *Death is for others.* She picked up the red candle and pressed it to the sitting room's curtains, setting them alight. She then set it down on its side among the wreckage of Jim's poisoned tantrum. Flame fairies danced and sang and praised Embla as she exited. She smiled despite herself.

"What was all that?" Cicero asked, watching the fire spread.

"P-poetry." Cillian spat despite his adoration.

He clung to his maker like a drunkard. Embla trudged past with a newfound sense of purpose. The drone piloted by Chief Harris hummed high overhead.

"The idiot is correct. Let's get back to the slaughter."

9

"There're so many plot holes, man! Dax protested. "How has this shit gone on for so long, for one. For two, how and why did you organize a coup despite how lucrative this set up is, and how in the hell has it not been uncovered?"

"Your last point was a reiteration of your first point," Aunt Gretta said, nearly draining another bottle of Riesling.

"Love," Uncle Lucas began as he gently guided her wine hand to the dresser. "I need you to be functional for the escape. I know things are absolutely out of hand, but you need to—*I need you*—to help Lilly."

"What are you talking about, Lucas?" Aunt Gretta asked. As soon as Uncle Lucas' hand left hers, she raised the glass back to her mouth and drank deeply. Uncle Lucas avoided her question and her defiance and addressed his guest.

"How *this shit*, as you say, has gone on for so long … well, up until modern times it wasn't an issue. People vanished all the time. Forensics started to get rid of the sacrifices—"

"Ew! I can't believe I never knew about this," Lee-Lee interjected.

"—got more complicated," Uncle Lucas continued. "Lee, your mother couldn't stand it. I couldn't stand it. Your grandfather was sick of it. But like any legacy, it's not easy to just stop. Especially if that legacy involves an entire town, countless riches, and *fucking vampires!* Grandpa planted the seeds of guilt and retribution when we were young. Did you know you had another uncle? My older brother, Roman. He was so skillful and kind. He was the best of us. I was the troubled middle child. Your mother … well, Tabitha was the magical one. She had a gift of light and laughter. You remind me so much of her, you know that?"

"She hated every penny you sent us," Lee-Lee glowered. "She treated every check you sent like a smallpox blanket."

"And yet, she never hesitated to deposit a single one," Uncle Lucas stated with a touch more bitterness than intended.

"Look, nothing in the history of this town or its residents is black and white. Houses have turned against the Pact in the past, but as you can see, nothing has changed. My father stood up to Cicero. He said he wouldn't participate in the slaughter anymore. He promised that he wouldn't say anything, just that he would no longer pay tribute. At that time, every household in Pacton had enough money that no one would have to work for at least three hundred years. Sure, the restaurants, the fire department, the shops—all part of the ploy.

Anyway, Cicero held my father while his cronies turned Roman–who was named after Cicero's birthplace as an homage–into one of them. We all sat in silent horror as we watched Roman gasp his last breath, like a diver about to jump into the ocean. His body convulsed violently, then slumped lifeless in their arms. The woman—Nordic bitch—Embla, bit into her wrist and grinded it into his mouth while we all muffled our terror. Nothing happened for what seemed like a lifetime of traumatic minutes, and then Roman's body began to convulse like he was being electrocuted. A roar curdled from his mouth and his eyes were cataract white. He lunged at your mother like a feral dog. Cicero snagged his ankle and pulled him back. Roman's claws gouged the wood floor, leaving deep tracks of splintered wood. He lifted my brother up by the throat and inspected him like he was at a thrift store. All the while, Roman railed against him in a supernatural rage. That's the only way I can describe it. Shrieking, clawing, kicking, flailing. Like a cat dangling by the collar from an indifferent branch."

"Your uncle likes similes," Jessie stated as he rubbed the Ziplock packet of acid tabs like a worry stone. "Shit! See what I did there? Like? Similes?"

His interjection was met with a collective *shut the fuck up* look from the rest of the room.

"My bad, ingrates."

"Anyway," Uncle Lucas sighed and wiped a mournful tear from his eye.

He popped open another bottle of Riesling and took five big chugs from it.

"Roman didn't even scratch the old bastard, savage as he was. 'This sometimes happens,' Cicero told us. 'Pity, we would delight in a new family member.' Then he ripped Rome's head off and tossed it by our feet. His mouth still chattered, searching for blood. 'You'll want to keep his body away from his head until dawn,' Cicero said with a smirk. He looked at my father and asked, 'The tithe continues, yes?' My father nodded through trembles of terror and grief. It wasn't the time for a hero."

"And now is?" Dax asked.

"Absolutely fucking not!" Uncle Lucas roared. "None of this shit would be happening if you didn't come here! We've been planning! Setting things in motion, so that in three more years we can *maybe* stand a chance at taking these bastards down!"

"So, another Halloween of murder and payouts?" Lee-Lee scoffed.

"Yes, Lilly, that's right. For the bigger picture. I hate it. I've always hated it. Your mother left, and I was so happy she could—even though it was only because I took the mantle of burden once my parents died— which for your grandfather, wasn't long after watching his son's head and torso ignite in the morning light after already watching him die and come back a feral creature. His heart couldn't take it. Your grandmother was much stronger. She played the game while strategizing with other weary households. You have to understand, this plan isn't new, it took decades to galvanize. And now it's ruined."

"How has this not been found out?" Lee-Lee asked.

Her mind spiraled with images of her family that she'd only seen in pictures. She never knew about her uncle Roman. It made sense that her mother never brought it up—too many painful questions.

"Yeah," Dax added. "In the land of guilty until proven innocent, how'd these monsters last this long without getting caught? We've seen their work; there isn't a house here didn't look like the basement of *Dead Alive* at one point."

"Tabula Rasa Cleaners, LLC," Aunt Gretta grunted. "Lucas already told you about them. They come, they clean, they scrub, they incinerate, they digitally manipulate, they leave."

"Whoa," Jessie gasped, watching Aunt Gretta's words exit her mouth like the fragrance emanating from a cartoon pie on a windowsill.

"Exactly," Uncle Lucas nodded, unaware that the exclamation wasn't about the current situation.

"Government officials, Hollywood elite, billionaires with private islands, all have that company on speed dial. Their record is impeccable. You could bomb an orphanage, and they would scrub all evidence except what could point to a faulty valve in the furnace. They'd hack any camera that would be in a five-mile radius and manipulate the footage to seem like everything was kosher. You could literally set off a bomb in Times Square, and they would make it seem like a gas leak. I've seen it. I've seen the footage of gratified visitors leaving their B&B and driving out of town while we knew full well that they were being incinerated at Swans funeral home across town. Sometimes the feds find an abandoned vehicle. Sometimes they discover the remnants of a family crashed into a ditch and somehow caught fire. A fire that has rendered anything but dental identification impossible."

"Nah, man," Dax folded his arms. "So many missing—no matter how—can't go unnoticed like that."

"You'd be correct," Uncle Lucas worriedly turned his attention back to the monitors. "If it wasn't Tabula Rasa. Itineraries, plane tickets, credit cards use at gas pumps … all manipulated."

"Could I hire them to change who I went to junior prom with?" Jessie chuckled. "I wanted to go with Dana Shultz but ended up climbing a tree with my buddy Matt and drinking his father's gin."

"Anyway, that's how it's been able to last as long as it has. Too many diabolically-complicit cogs in an ancient murder machine." Uncle Lucas sighed.

"He is totally writing our next album," Jessie grinned.

"Lucas!" Chief Harris' voice crackled through the HAM radio.

"Go for Lucas, Chief!"

"Over," Jessie added.

"Shut up!" Uncle Lucas growled.

"Over," Jessie added.

"They're at the Goreman house! They're about to wreak havoc on a douchebag wedding or whatever, over."

"So what do we do? Over?" Uncle Lucas asked, worryingly eyeing his wife.

"Get a fucking move on!"

Uncle Lucas moved swiftly to the armoire and pressed a hidden button on the right side, causing it to click loudly. Then, he pushed it with ease to the left, revealing a hidden stairwell. He ushered Lee-Lee and Dax to the exit. Aunt Gretta hesitated. He also noticed Jessie trying to shove the bag of acid tabs under the door to the hallway.

"The hell are you doing, kid?"

"They want acid, I'll give it to them!" Jessie exclaimed. "They can see all the sunshine colors and whatever bullshit murderous nocturnal fuckwads see when they're tripping nut sacks."

"That's not how it works, I'm afraid," Uncle Lucas said while snatching the baggie from Jessie. "It needs to be in the blood. Everything else gets rejected. It's always the blood."

"Then let them have me!" Jessie tried in vain to snatch the baggie back. "I'm a godforsaken accordion-slash-triangle player in a band with a fucking *terrible* name—"

"—Fuck your mouth, Jess," Dax interrupted.

"This ain't the time for heroics, and there's not a damn thing wrong with our name."

"Whatever, Dax … even if your head is a skull with a Santa hat, let me do something that does some good for once!"

"Kids!" Uncle Lucas warned as he opened a dresser drawer. He produced a thick roll of money. "You all have potential. You get out of this fucking mess, and you can do anything. Take this …" He tossed the roll to Lee-Lee. "If I don't make it, expect a hefty payday for you and your mother. And Jessie? Here, take your drugs back and get the hell out of here. Gretta knows the way … right, love? Right, left, right, straight, right?"

"You better get whatever it is *in* your head the hell *out*!" Aunt Gretta protested. "We can all leave now—*right* now. No need to play martyr, like Drax said."

"Dax. It's Dax …"

"Whatever. There's no reason to stay behind. Don't you *dare* think of leaving me!"

"Technically, my love, you're the one leaving," Uncle Lucas smiled and began to cry. "This is it for us, babe. I have a lot to answer for, and I can buy you all much more time than our young friend could. Dax, please help my wife down the spiral stairs that leads to the escape hatch?" He pulled his wife close and kissed her as passionately as they used to when their love was young and unburdened by guilt.

"Yessir, Uncle Lucas. Please, Ma'am, let's go." Dax placed a hand on her shoulder, but she shrugged it off.

"We should either go together or *go* together," Aunt Gretta stated, cold as ice. "This sacrifice nonsense is ridiculous."

Uncle Lucas kissed her on the forehead then

held her at arm's length.

"You're right, darling, as always. Let's finish the plan together and get the hell out. Dax? If you would … I'll lock the bookcase behind us."

"On it. Come on, Ma'am," Dax ushered her to the opening and then down the stairs. She was so relieved that she didn't object at all. Jessie managed to find the railing before he fell. Lee-Lee lingered.

"You're not coming with us, are you?"

Uncle Lucas just shook his head.

"I'm tired of carrying you, kid. Piss off and live."

He winked and turned his attention back to the security monitors. Lee-Lee scowled with the regret that she was the reason all this was happening. Perhaps not the centuries of murder but fouling the plan to end it. Lee-Lee descended the iron spiral stairs and met the others at the submarine-looking hatch. They heard the soft scraping of the armoire closing above and looked at each other with unease when they heard the sharp clack of the lock.

"No! You bastard!"

Aunt Gretta ripped herself from Dax's grip and clambered up the spiral staircase. She pounded on the back of the armoire until her hands ached.

"Don't you fucking do this, Lucas! You don't need to die to avenge your family!"

"No," Uncle Lucas' voice said softly through the barrier. "But right now? I'm only interested in keeping the family I still have alive. Be quick and be quiet. I love you, UnforGrettable … until the stars fall from the sky."

"I'm too old to start dating, you inconsiderate prick!" Aunt Gretta said.

They shared a soft, bittersweet chuckle. Partaking in a lifetime of wretched horror together tends to make a couple … peculiar.

"Nonsense! You've got plenty of mileage left on that hot box. Go make some muscly pool boy happy."

"Love you, idiot," Aunt Gretta sniffled.

"Stars and all, baby. Now please go."

Aunt Gretta wiped the tears from her eyes and steeled herself.

"Drax? Let's get this over with."

"Really?" Dax objected.

"Let's get this over with, Drax!" Lee-Lee joked despite her sadness. "Sorry, babe, I couldn't resist."

"Pssh, whatever."

Dax sucked his teeth then twisted the bulkhead. He lifted the metal hub, releasing the horrid stench of sewage and rot. Everyone recoiled except Jessie, who saw blacklight butterflies rising as if caught in a tornado. Dax shook the stink from his nostrils and chuckled softly to himself.

"Hey, Lee … remember when we were on tour with Spooge Puma, and we were playing at The Ookie Cookie, and someone sabotaged the toilets, and the floor was getting creepingly covered by beer and chicken wing shit? And you thought that was our lowest point, and I said, 'don't worry baby, it could always get worse'?"

"Not really?" Lee-Lee shrugged.

"Well … either way, I was right."

10

"You look tense, my love."

Embla clasped her murderous hand around Cicero's left arm while they surveyed the Goreman house. They watched the assembly of sinning livestock—within and without—scurrying and cavorting to deny their miniscule, and various mortal afflictions.

The LSD had already started to subside, much to her chagrin. She had rather enjoyed the experience.

"Tonight has been a cavalcade of follies and deceit. Our welcome and mutual prosperity has been tested. It mystifies and vexes me that anyone within Pacton would sully such a lucrative treaty."

Cicero's attention turned inward.

"You haven't been mortal for ages, my darling," Embla said softly. "You may have forgotten how mercurial the cattle consciousness can be. For instance, look to our beautiful, Celtic idiot, see how his conscience has served him tonight."

Her attention turned back to the Goreman house. The after-wedding party guests of YouTube's latest millionaire (and completely-lacking-in-talent influencer) Brett Beezermann—a.k.a. "The Beez"—and his new bride, Onlyfans' trending-for-two-weeks Eden Nova, traipsed around the property like so many ants. *No*, Embla thought. *Ants have an actual purpose. These are just parasites.*

Her thoughts raced back to the many English monasteries where she stood with her Viking comrades—though in reality, her captors—against paltry priests and townsfolk. The victims thought that the Vikings were a punishment from God, which pleased Embla. The Christian god was a triviality in her eyes. A usurper. Each monastery was populated by boy-buggers and misogynists begging for the blade. The churches in France were no different. The same affronts to decency but in another language. This particular abbey, however, seemed quite different from when last their oars had rested. There were no bells. No screams. No indication that the fools inside knew their doom had come ashore.

"Something is wrong," Bjorn Erikson, the raid chief, stated while he fidgeted with his chin braid.

He, too, had grown accustomed to the panic that led to the slaughter. There were no archers, nor pitchfork-wielding peasants to greet them. Not a single imploring bastard in robes to entreat the heathen horde.

"Perhaps the pathetic godmen saw the folly in resisting and saved us the pleasure of slaughtering them ourselves," the Berserker named Arne shrugged the bear pelt on his massive shoulders. "We have been building quite a reputation along these shores."

"I've heard suicide is a sin to these people," Embla ridiculed. "This makes sense to me. Live in abject squalor and die penniless and without honor. If you dare take control of your own fate, look forward to the never-ending torture of hell."

"Hel?" Arne asked. "These Christians believe in our ways?"

"Not exactly," Embla scoffed. "They pillage and plunder stories and make them their own, much like we do with their ill-gotten riches. There's nothing they say that hasn't already been uttered."

"You know a lot for a slave girl," Bjorn smirked. "Well, I am of the mind to plunder the riches within, then set this church ablaze in the name of the older gods. Let us proceed!" Bjorn raised his ax to the cheer of his squad of seasoned raiders.

"I was a noblewoman once," Embla snarled, which caused Bjorn to laugh.

"Yes indeed—the inheritress to a paltry fishing port governed by a goat's nutsack of a jarl. My father *owned* your father, Little Wolf. Loathe am I to reiterate, when it came down to offering his daughter—*you*—or be obliterated, your pathetic father did not hesitate. It's only because I could see your shieldmaiden potential that you're here and not another of my father's cum catchers."

"Agreed, I would loathe to be like your mother … what was her name? There are so many of those catchers … which one was yours?"

Embla's smirk was short lived. Bjorn took her by the throat and pulled her close with a growl. She instinctively clutched the handle of one of her daggers to slide between his ribs but paused when Arne bellowed a mighty laugh. The rest of the twenty-five strong laughed along with him.

"Little Wolf has fangs!" Arne laughed.

This caused Bjorn to let her go. It would be in poor taste to look so petty, though he was within his rights to do as he pleased with his property. His fingers moved from her throat to her left shoulder. Her fingers moved altogether from the dagger's grip.

"Very well, *Little Wolf*, you may have the honor of taking point. Don't worry, we'll be *right* behind you."

Bjorn gave her a little shove. The full moon's light caused deep shadows and harsh luminosity along the inclined path from the shore to the monastery.

The trees look like sentries, Embla thought as she crept.

The night was so still and silent that the only sounds she could hear were those of her feet. Bjorn and his men moved slowly below, at his order of course. She would brave any traps or ambushes alone as punishment for her insolence. Arne had other ideas. He trudged the hill with a grin so big Embla could see it in both shadow and light. He kept his axe sheathed to keep the moonlight from glinting off the blade. Embla slowed her pace to let the massive man catch up.

"Little Wolf and Big Bear!" Arne chuckled softly. "What adventure shall we have this night? Ambush? All-out battle with tiny men in robes?"

"What of Bjorn's orders?" Embla asked.

Arne simply scoffed.

"I've known that brat since he was slick from his mother's purse. What will he do, give me a spanking? I'd like to see him try! He … likes you, you know…"

"He has a strange way of expressing it," Embla sneered.

"I feel you will earn your freedom yet."

The darkened place of worship loomed like a massive headstone against the starless sky.

"Hm. A bad omen," Arne mused.

As they made it to the monastery doors, Arne waved to the others halfway down the path that it was safe to continue.

"The doors aren't barred," Embla stated, pushing the right side of the big wooden doors open.

Arne lightly pushed her aside so he could enter first. He drew his bearded ax and motioned with his head to follow.

The chapel was a silent tomb, devoid of any hint that life had ever been present. The raiders stealthily filed in and waited for orders. Bjorn lit his torch and held it high. Several others did the same. Soon, the large chapel shadows danced.

"Looks to be deserted," Arne said with a tinge of disappointment.

"Hm. Perhaps they're slumbering." Bjorn offered, drawing his sword.

"Perhaps they are all *dead*."

A voice boomed from all around. They tried to locate the source of the strange sounding voice, but Embla remembered how chapel acoustics worked from past raids.

"The altar!" she shouted.

All eyes focused on the yawning darkness of the altar where the torch lights could not reach—and on the cobalt eyes that pierced it.

"I asked Nox for more cattle, and my goddess has delivered yet again! My sincerest apologies if I am butchering your native tongue, my good heathens. Norse has always been bitter on my lips."

"Sven," Bjorn nodded to his archer, who sent an arrow true without hesitation.

The shimmering eyes did not blink.

"Worth a try…" spoke the darkness.

"Try this!" Arne shouted and charged into the black with his ax held at the ready.

He roared as he swung and vanished into the yearning void. The room fell silent, save for shifting feet and clinking armor then the whimpering that came from the altar that comingled with deep gulping.

"Light the torches!" Bjorn ordered.

Several torch-bearing raiders rushed to light the torches fixed to the wall sconces on either side of the nave. Light swiftly surged over the pews and crashed into the pulpit where Cicero—still looking mostly human—embraced Arne like a lover.

The group gasped at the sight of the bloodied maw that grinned and their comrade's head which only had the spinal cord keeping it from falling to the planks below. Bjorn gave the order to attack, and to the delight of the fiend at the altar, the raiders charged. Cicero threw Arne's limp corpse with the impact of a falling tree, crushing two warriors. In a dazzling flurry of motion, the vampire gracefully evaded each attack as he entered the thick of battle. Arms that still clutched swords and axes soared to the rafters and the windows like startled brush fowl. Cicero laughed as heads were crushed and sternums caved in by his effortless strikes. Some he would not kill—only cripple—so that he could feed once the amusement came to an end. The slaughter only lasted a minute and a half.

Embla stood at the butchery's edge, her daggers at the ready. Despite the terror that coiled around her heart like the Midgard Serpent, her eyes were fierce and focused.

Behind her, Bjorn trembled.

"*Little Wolf* …" Cicero spoke with a smile.

His voice pierced the agonizing cries of the few left alive. "There is fire behind your eyes. A passion. You are of nobility, that I can see as clearly as the brightest star. The cowering wretch behind you isn't worth his weight in sparrow shit. Join me and never again know the subjugation of servitude."

"You know I am a slave?" Embla asked, taken

aback.

The vampire's fang-filled smile grew even wider.

"I heard that low-born swine saying as such after the last oar's splash. This is but one of the gifts I can give to you. Your senses will be that of a god. No man will stand above you. Your only master will be the hunger. But we have plenty in which to sup."

"Y-you'll l-lose your soul, Embla!" Bjorn uttered.

"And to whom would she give her soul? Where would she place it? Can one lose a soul when one cannot die? No, cattle. Her iron-forged soul would still be hers. What say you, child?"

"I will not become a monster!" Embla roared and lunged.

Her daggers spun and swiped and thrusted, but her target always seemed to just be a whisper too far. Cicero savored her graceful animosity. Even more so when her blade caressed his right cheek just below his eye, causing the faintest sting and droplet of ancient blood. Cicero gasped with delight.

"You already *are* a monster, Little Wolf—I simply offer you the chance to show the world."

Cicero unfurled the fingers of his right hand towards Embla. Her mind and heart raced. She knew the Norns had woven greatness into her story—could *this* be that thread? She slid her daggers into their sheathes and placed her hand in his. Both looked to the clanging door where Bjorn had run in terror.

"What must I do?" asked Embla. Cicero pulled her close. She smelled copper and autumn leaves.

"Allow my graveyard kiss … then kiss me back," Cicero winked.

Embla nodded. Gently, the vampire sank his fangs into her neck and began to drink. Embla marveled at how little the pain was. It almost tickled—a tingle much like a limb falling asleep. The chapel began to spin as she swooned from blood loss. The torch light danced across her darkening vision, and she could feel Cicero's arms effortlessly hold her as her legs gave out. Their eyes met, and then blackness.

When Embla awoke, her mouth was pressed to Cicero's neck. His artery pumped liquid sweeter than any mead into her eager mouth. As she gulped, her body tingled like a thousand fireflies were dancing throughout. She didn't want that feeling to ever end. Cicero gently removed her face from his neck and laughed softly as she struggled to latch back on.

"I want m-more!" Embla growled between the final gulps.

"And more you shall have, my dear …" he held her by the arms like a parent would a rambunctious child. "Once your transformation has concluded we shall feed."

Embla's body began to shudder violently. Every vein in her body wanted to burst from her hardening skin. Her gums itched intensely as her mortal teeth fell out to make way for thirty-two fangs of various sizes that pushed through. She howled in agony.

"This is that last pain you will ever feel, I promise. It will be over soon."

Cicero's countenance changed from concern to contentment once Embla fell silent and looked upon him with shimmering silver eyes.

"Come on—come on!" Bjorn cried out as he attempted to push the ship's bow into the water. The screams from the church had stopped, and he was unsure whether or not that was a good thing. He strained against the hull again to no avail.

"You're going to die tired if you keep that up,"

Embla said, several yards up the hill. Bjorn spun to face her. The moon was now above the monastery, causing Embla to be backlit. He could only see her piercing eyes clearly.

"Y-you escaped? *Ha-Ha*!" Bjorn's laugh was near-manic. "C-come and help me unmoor the ship and-and we will—*you will* be free! I'll grant it! M-my father c-can go to Hel!"

Embla closed the distance between them in a heartbeat. She barely managed to stop before smashing into her former master. With her newfound preternatural strength, she took hold of Bjorn's braided ponytail and pulled his face close to her dagger grin.

"And so he shall. But, you first …"

Embla's laughter danced above Bjorn's screams as she dragged him by the hair up the hill and back into the monastery, closing the door behind them.

11

"I once was beautiful …" Embla said softly to a burly man in a tee-shirt two sizes too small.

He stood with his arms folded across his chest like a bouncer in front of a club. He sneered at the sight of Embla's now ancient visage.

"I got some bad news for ya, bitch. Either your makeup is top-fucking-shelf, or someone beat yo ass mercilessly with the futt bugly stick!"

"Oh-ho! You should *not* have said that peasant!" Cicero chuckled. The burly man puffed his chest.

"You elitist motherfu—" the man began but was cut off by Embla's hand to his throat.

She slammed him face first onto the storm drain. For a moment, his eyes met those of Aunt Gretta below. Then Embla smashed her foot down hard. Blood, skull, brains, teeth, and eyes smooshed forcefully through the grating and showered Aunt Gretta. Dax rushed to her and placed his hand over her mouth before she could scream. She tore his hand from her slick face and spit an eye and three teeth into the sewer water. Aunt Gretta shoved Dax away and moved herself from the gushing blood from above. She placed a finger to her mouth to signal silence. Once the screaming had begun filling the night, she ushered the group onward.

"*Pffhuh*!" she spat again. "We're nearly at the station … we've been down here too long."

"Probably the safest place to be," Lee-Lee said softly.

"Yeah, why don't we just stay put?" Jesse asked as they walked carefully on the slippery concrete path.

"Because they always check the sewers for hideaways. And if we somehow managed to stay clear of *them*, come morning, the cleaners will have set the tunnels on fire. I refuse to die down here. So, let's all shut our mouths and keep going. Straight."

They nodded and continued silently on.

The three vampires rampaged through the Goreman house as though they were children in a toy store.

Cillian fed deeply in order to fully purge his system of the poison he so shamefully ingested at the Cobbler house. His foolish heart still beat a faint but noticeably human rhythm. He wasn't nearly as strong as the others–and they often reminded him of it. In time, though, his flesh will become harder and his disposition even more so. He was still an acolyte in their eyes, not an equal, which caused him to be gratuitously ferocious. Gunfire erupted from several partygoers, causing even more panic. A round struck Cillian in the shoulder, and he shrieked in pain.

"Oh, shit! We can hurt them!" the partygoer cheered, then fired his weapon without any noticeable skill, striking several in the stampeding crowd instead of his intended target.

Cicero had taken the upper floors while Embla stalked those who ran from the house, leaving Cillian on his own. Bullets from other partygoers struck the emerald-eyed monster, causing his legs to give out. The man approached Cillian and placed the gun to his forehead.

"You picked the wrong house, cocksucker!"

Cillian grasped the man's hand and squeezed it until metal and bone were entangled. He then pulled the mortal to him and sank his fangs deep into his throat. The bullets clinked on the wood floor as they were expelled from Cillian's body. His rampage resumed.

Upstairs, Mr. and Mrs. Goreman fucked furiously to the sounds of slaughter coming from beyond the safety of their suite. Monitors, much like those in the Allore house, displayed the carnage in HD. The Goremans thought about the vast sum of money they would receive come morning, and the sheer contempt they had for the younger generation currently getting eviscerated, and they climaxed together.

Embla pulled her nightmare mouth from the nape of another *too-narcissistic-and-stupid-to-be-useful-in-real-life* internet influencer and sighed. Her system purged itself of the LSD, stripping the vibrant colors from the night sky and gushing blood and slithering entrails. She scanned the landscape for runners, but only mutilated corpses remained. She huffed then walked into the house. Cillian sat on the couch like he was watching the game after a Thanksgiving meal.

"Feeling any better?" Embla asked.

"I am. The poison has been flushed from my system. Thank you for your concern. Quite a surprise."

"I wasn't concerned; I simply wanted to know if I would have to nail you to the roof so sunrise would rid us of your idiocy."

"Now, Embla …" Cicero descended the stairs with the betrotheds' wrists in his iron grip. "If I did not know better, I would say it sounds like you're developing feelings for our peculiar poet."

"P-please let us go," Eden Nova pleaded.

"No." Cicero replied.

"You brought us dessert, darling?" Embla grinned. Cillian lifted himself from the couch and they approached.

"No, my loves … we have unfinished business with Lucas Allore. While we must adhere to the pact, these two do not."

"Wh-what are you talkin' about, man?" Brett Beezermann creaked as he surveyed the scores of dead. He vomited as he cried. "Wuh-we have money, man! We can puh-pay you—make you rich, maaaan!"

"We've spent more riches than you could ever earn simply for the delight of killing you all tonight. If you'd like to live a while longer, I suggest you do our bidding."

"We help you and you let us live?" Eden asked.

"Assist us in this endeavor and you have my word that you will be allowed to leave that house in peace."

Cicero attempted a reassuring grin, but that only caused more dread in the young couple.

"These should suffice in their task," Embla handed the couple two heraldic axes that had crisscrossed above the fireplace mantle. "They are decorative but heavy enough."

"They will do. Come now, let us get to the crux

of this evening's treachery."

Cicero nodded and led the group outside where more visual trauma awaited Brett and Eden.

"Oh. My. GOD! Everyone's dead!" Eden cried.

"More than dead, darling," Embla grinned. "They have become art."

"He owed me twenty grand!" Brett groaned as he stepped over a friend.

Across the empty street and up the hill they went, the moon receding slightly behind the Allore house, as though hiding its eyes from the horrors down below. The house was quiet and peaceful. Eden and Brett had no idea about the carnage down the hall. They were ushered up the large staircase and to Uncle Lucas' suite. Cicero ran his index finger along his chin and wiped a streak of blood from it. With the blood he marked the door with an X.

"Strike here."

"Question … why can't you do it?" Brett asked.

"Because of that," Cillian pointed to the sigil on the door.

"A bunch of squiggles? *Pffft!*" Eden ridiculed. It took Embla's entire might not to cave Eden's skull in right then and there.

"A sigil holds more power than you can—" Cillian began to explain but was cut short by Cicero's raised hand.

"They needn't a lesson on magics, my dear. They need only to swing those axes. And do try to hit the mark, would you?"

Cicero backed away from the door and the couple began their work. The door's paint barely scuffed under the feebleness of their strikes.

"*Ungh*!" Eden grunted as the axe bounced off the door and from her grip.

"Pick it up, slag!" Embla ordered. "Where did you two learn to swing axes, eh? Pathetic!"

"Listen, bitch—I suck dick on camera for money! I'm not a fucking lumberjack!"

"And what of you, big boy?" Embla turned her attention to Brett. "Are those muscles under that oversized shirt, or rolling hills of lard?"

"Your words hurt, ma'am," Brett frowned.

Embla moved behind him and turned his head to look at Eden.

"Swing the axe as hard as your arteries or I'll pop your little whore's head off like a daffodil."

"*Or*, we don't do a fucking thing, and you don't get through the door—how about that?"

Eden puffed her chest and sneered. Cicero gently cradled her face with his bloodied fingers.

"I never lose, child …" he whispered. "Not a single moment in history have I given up or failed to accomplish my goal despite insurmountable odds. I always find a way. Always. Now, I have been extremely generous in giving you the opportunity to leave this house alive, have I not? You do this small task for us, and I promise your freedom. Otherwise? I will break your spines so that you cannot move, then burn the house down with you in it. I simply wanted to speak with the turncoat on the other side of this door, but It's not the end of the world if I do not. The end of your world, yes, but not mine."

"O-okay," Eden nodded meekly, and the couple began to strike the door again.

"We're going to be here a while … unless *someone wants to open the door for us, eh*?" Embla shouted to Uncle Lucas.

"Go fuck yourself, Viking bitch!" Uncle Lucas

replied.

Embla responded with a hiss.

"There's no need for the three of us to wait here," Cicero said. "Go and see if there are any stragglers to hunt."

His companions bowed their heads then darted back into the night. Cicero turned his attention back to the two pathetic representatives of the human species and sighed.

12

"Here it is! We've made it!" Aunt Gretta excitedly whispered as she pointed to a ladder that led to a large metal cover.

She hurried through the puddles on the walkway, making more sound than she should have, but she didn't care. Soon they would be dry, warm, and safe from the prospect of a brutal death.

"Drax, get up there and open the hatch!"

"Why do you think it's okay to order the black man around, huh, Auntie?" Dax squared his shoulders.

"Don't be an idiot," Aunt Gretta scoffed and rolled her eyes. "Look at you then look at our alternative."

She pointed at Jessie, who cradled his accordion like a newborn.

"Thanks for completely overlooking me … *Auntie*," Lee-Lee shook her head.

"When you put it that way, I apologize," Dax said with a twinge of awkwardness.

He clambered up the metal ladder and attempted to turn the circular handle. It wouldn't budge.

"There's a panel to the right of the wheel, young man," Police Chief Harris' voice came from a callbox at the mouth of the ladder's alcove, startling everyone.

"Jesus rat-fucking Christ, Sam!" Aunt Gretta shouted, her voice echoing through the tunnels.

She then noticed the CCTV camera on the other side of the water pointing at the alcove. Its red light blinked steadily. "If you knew we were coming, why didn't you—"

"Press the red button, Gretta," Chief Harris said. "Can't hear you 'less you press the button. Once you're done speaking, let it go, then it's my turn again."

Aunt Gretta huffed as she pressed the button.

"There, better? Why didn't you leave the hatch unlocked if you knew we were coming?"

"Had a … complication. Couldn't get to it. Big fella at the hatch? Slide the rectangle panel cover next to the wheel to the right. When you see the buttons, press one-seven-six-one then the green button with the checkmark."

"On it," Dax asserted and followed the directions.

The panel trilled and the locking mechanism thumped loudly. He turned the wheel clockwise until he heard the bolt click into place, then pushed the hatch up. He lifted himself into the precinct's garage, then helped the others up. Automatic motion-sensor lights *ting-ting-tinged* as they came on. The garage was completely empty except for a vehicle at the back that was covered in a tarp.

"This way." Aunt Gretta pointed to a door marked Lobby.

As she opened it, a stench of copper and feces struck them, much like the main floor of the Allore house. Death reached the police station before the survivors did.

"Oh, fuck! What if they're still here?" Lee-Lee froze at the threshold.

"Sam wouldn't have let us in—now come on, Lee, move it!" Aunt Gretta said sternly.

"Unless he's working *for* them …" Jessie stated more to himself than to anyone else.

The hallway was decorated with pictures of past lawmen, unsurprisingly with the same last name. Each face they passed looked wearier and less righteous than the one before. Evidently, the lucrative bounty on selling your fellow man out to ungodly sadists took a generational toll on those who swore to protect and serve.

The lobby had a standard, small-town station layout and was decorated for Halloween with hanging cloth ghosts, plastic jack-o-lanterns, and a bashed-in body by the intake counter. Blood and chunks of brain-gunked hair had splashed like fireworks on the middle section of the polycarbonate window that ran the entire length of the counter, essentially sealing the lobby from the room beyond. In that room was where Chief Sam Harris and his guest stood solemnly by the desks. A scruffy mutt with a skull bandana around its neck stood at attention and wagged its tail excitedly at the newcomers.

Lee-Lee noticed that the room had cots, a refrigerator and even a latrine. These two had no intention of going anywhere, and she couldn't blame them. The station lobby was small (compared to those Lee-Lee had been escorted through a few times for *artistic expression*). To the left of the intake counter was a payphone, snack and beverage vending machines, a table with a Keurig and cups, and a door that led to the offices and cells. It seemed a bit underwhelming for such a touristy town.

"The hell happened, Sam?" Aunt Gretta asked, trying not to get too close to the window.

Sam approached the cleaner portion of the window and sighed.

"They just left here …" Sam said, shaking his head. "They're on their 'Last Scraps' run. Just two of them, though—the female and the younger one. Don't know where their boss is."

"Last Scraps?" Dax asked.

"Stragglers, son. They hunt for those who might have snuck away during the chaos and hid or ran. They followed this poor sonovabitch in here and used him like a battering ram against the glass. That's why his head and upper body are paste."

"What are those clean streaks on the glass?" Lee-Lee asked, knowing she'd regret it.

"That's where they licked," Sam replied with a frown. "They knew they couldn't break the glass like that; they did it just to fuck with us."

"Terrible as that is, Sam, you can go on ahead and let us in."

Aunt Gretta pointed to the door at the other side of the sealed room.

"Buzz us through the door and we'll meet you at the one with the sigil."

Sam looked shamefully to the floor.

"Afraid I can't do that, Gretta," he replied with pain in his voice.

"You better be joking, Sam!" Aunt Gretta's eyes grew wide with building rage.

"Wish I was, hun, really. Mr. Powell and I were getting ready to head to the roof to do another drone run when we saw the now deceased fellah running towards the door. I knew he was a last scrap and couldn't risk the plan going all to hell, so I … I sealed us in."

"You knew we were coming!" Aunt Gretta hammered her fist on the glass.

"I know! I'm sorry! I couldn't risk it! We've got a ton of evidence to show the world, Gretta. Mr. Powell here thinks he could set things in motion to finally stop this goddamn abomination of a town. Maybe even get those bloodsucking bastards dragged into the light! Imagine that? We'd be free of the pact!"

"You'd all still have to answer for your part in it," Dax stated. "Stopping this doesn't absolve you of a fucking thing."

"You're right, son … and I'm okay with that. Those on board, like Miss Lilly's aunt and uncle are okay with it, too. It's gotta end, and we gotta end it. Would have been a smooth execution if you didn't swing into town and throw a wrench in the goddamn works, but here we are."

Sam stood at a stocky six-foot-one, and had a full mustache as was befitting the archetype of a small-town cop. His frame was heavy but not entirely fat. His chest and arms were thick with muscle, but his belly was rounded by beer and bourbon. His counterpart stood four inches shorter and was athletically thin under his shirt and tie.

"So, you're the reporter Sam told me was the best?"

"The best might be a bit much, but I've been known to get results, yeah. The name is Parker Powell," he replied.

His voice was deep and sandy, belying his youthful demeanor. He had dusty-blond unkempt hair, round wire-rimmed glasses, and a kind smile under three days' worth of stubble.

"You did that piece about Gravenfrost, didn't you?" Lee-Lee asked, genuinely intrigued.

Dax shot her a look of confusion.

"What? I read. Especially about places we're booked to play at … *were* booked … to …"

Tears welled up in her eyes. Dax pulled her in gently for a hug. Shock had begun to rear its head.

"That your dog?" Dax asked, trying to change the subject. "Scrappy-looking fella."

"Yeah, this is Bukowski."

Powell gave the dog a noggin rub.

"He's my road homie. Funny enough, we also met in Gravenfrost."

"What was that place there called? The one we were gonna play at?" Dax asked Lee-Lee.

"I don't remember … something crab?"

"Crab Meat Sally's," Jessie stated as he stared out the front door into the night. "Their slogan is 'Sally's got Crabs'."

"How do you remember this random shit?" Dax chuckled despite his own feelings of terror.

"S'what I do. And the triangle. And acid."

Jessie didn't take his eyes from the vacant street. His thoughts turned back to the dilemma at hand. They weren't safe. They weren't prepared to fight. They also weren't prepared to die. Well, the others weren't, by his estimation. Jessie, on the other hand, had the entire cosmos open before him. Time and space were con-structs of a slave culture. A punishment beset upon ourselves for reasons no one remembers until they shed their mortality and reconnect with The Source. Why would anyone volunteer for such a prison of rot? To feel perfection again upon dying—that must be it. An eternity of bliss is akin to nothing if not juxtaposed to pain and loss. Even the greatest pleasure can become banal if always present. It could even become a torment in and of itself. There's the crux. Detach from The Source and suffer the flesh until it is—for lack of a better word—*time* to reconnect and feel the delight of totality once more.

"You know what you have to do, Jessie," Alan Sparklemane, The Unicorn said.

He stood so large and radiant next to Jessie, who simply nodded.

"I know, Alan Sparklemane. I'll miss them, though."

"You *are* them, Jessie. And *they* are you. There is nothing to be missed. Think of it this way: Each of us is a wave that has risen from the same body of water. We rise individually yet once we've crested and crashed, we become the ocean once again."

"You are a wise and noble steed, my friend."

Jessie ran his fingers through the unicorn's mane, sending a shower of sparkles across the room.

Dax turned to look at his bandmate rubbing empty air.

"And you are a wise and noble friend. And one *hell* of a musician!" Alan Sparklemane whickered then shat a pile of steaming rainbow chunks.

"You always know just what to say …" Jessie smiled and dropped the crumpled, empty sheet of acid tabs to the floor.

"What are we meant to do, Sam?" Aunt Gretta asked with a defeated tone. "You won't let us in—"

"—*Can't* let you—" Sam interjected.

"Yeah, it's definitely the right time for semantics." Lee-Lee sneered.

"You won't let us in, those freaks are on the hunt, and we don't even have a dollar to get a goddamn candy bar from the machine over there," Dax said.

"Hhhh. Look …" Sam began.

He ran his hand over his freshly trimmed brown hair and sighed hard. He walked over to one of the desks closer to the sigil door and rummaged through the bug-out-bag on top of it. He produced several items from it and moved back to the window.

"You have three options. One, take these two tactical security flashlights fixed with ultraviolet bulbs and head to the roof to wait for dawn. Two, use these keys for the cruiser you saw in the garage…"

"The one under the tarp?" Dax asked. "That runs?"

"It does. It's been modified a bit. I've been working on it in the event that we have to go to war with the vamps—which I was hoping to avoid until next time. UV headlights, an oversized steel bull bar, and a shotgun in the trunk with silver/salt-packed rounds. Try to get out of town. Might be tricky because of the roadblocks we had to set up to keep travelers out and tributes in, though. The bull bar should come in handy with that."

"What's the third option?" Aunt Gretta asked, understandably impatient.

"Go back into the sewer and make your way to the Cobbler's house. They were already there, and I can't imagine they'd go back."

"You said they're on the hunt for scraps," Dax mentioned. "What makes you think they won't back track? Those motherfuckers move fast. And what's to say they won't check the sewers? Or the rooftops? Shit, man, the only option that makes sense is the getaway."

"Yeah," Lee-Lee agreed. "We have a fighting chance at least."

"Well, I think I'd rather wait it out on the roof," Aunt Gretta stated. "At the very least, I'll be close to Lucas when the sun comes up and this nightmare is over."

"Okay, take these at least before you make a decision."

Sam lifted the lid on a sliding drawer that connected the office with the lobby, and set the flashlights, car key, and two keys from his keyring inside. He pushed the drawer, so it slid towards the group.

"Those other two keys are for the vending machines. Take what you need."

"How does that not break the seal?" Lee-Lee asked.

"You can't lift the lid until I've pushed the drawer out all the way and the handle is set. At no time is there a gap. Same the other way around."

"Probably should have one of those for people, huh?" said Powell over his shoulder as he worked on his laptop. "Like they have in quarantine areas. I dunno, maybe something like that would work … anyway, after the drawer is free, push it back, please?"

"The drawer is for people to drop off drugs and firearms safely," Sam stated with some indignation. "It wasn't designed for this exactly."

"Get a lot of drugs and firearms in this town?"

Dax scoffed as he emptied the contents of the drawer.

"Aesthetics, I'm sure," nodded Powell. "After a few hundred years of kowtowing to undead knuckle-fuckers, I'm sure no one's thought much about helping their fellow man. But now's your chance, Chief—assuming any of us get to see sunrise. Here we go …"

Powell unplugged a portable hard drive from his laptop and brought it to the drawer.

"What's on that?" Lee-Lee asked.

Meanwhile, Dax had made his way to the vending machines and opened them up. Aunt Gretta locked the front door and shivered.

"Just about everything we've captured from the drone and CCTV cameras around town. Sam gave me access to the servers, so I soaked it all up. Some documents, too—those I had time to scan, at least. It's not everything, but it's a start. If you make it out, call the number on the card I taped to it. He's an asshole, but his heart is in the right place."

Powell set the hard drive into the drawer gently then pushed it to Lee-Lee.

"What about you? You not planning on making it out?"

"Of course I am," chuckled Powell. "But if you do and I don't? At least the Pacton Plan will continue, and this nightmare won't happen again."

"Great, now that that's all sorted, let's all settle down, settle in, and try to run out the clock." Sam said, then paused when he noticed Aunt Gretta shivering by the door.

"Gretta? Step away from the door, hun. There are some blankets and coats in the back that you can have, but I can't have you standing there in full view."

"O-okay …" Aunt Gretta replied.

Her adrenaline dipped and she felt the crash of post-fight-or-flight.

"Come on, Aunt Gretta, let's see what we can find."

Lee-Lee slid the long, metal flashlight into her waistband and ushered her aunt to the side door. Dax handed them a water bottle each and downed the contents of his own. Then it hit him.

"Hey … where the hell is Jessie?"

The decorative axe finally breached the saferoom door, sending shared of wood to the carpet. Uncle Lucas steeled himself and unsheathed the knife he kept on the nightstand. After a few more hacks the opening was large enough for Brett to reach inside for the dead-bolt.

Uncle Lucas slammed the knife down into Brett's forearm before he could undo the lock. Brett shrieked and attempted to pull his arm from the opening, but Uncle Lucas held tight. Cicero grabbed Brett's shoulders and yanked him from the door, causing the blade to pull all the way down his arm and free between his fingers. Brett screamed. Cicero pulled him close with a smile.

"Well done. You both are free to leave the house."

"Wh-what about my a-arm?" Brett howled in pain.

"Walk it off."

Cicero gave Brett a little shove, and he and Eden raced down the stairs. Cicero peeked through the opening at Uncle Lucas and licked his lips.

"Oh, my … door breach. I have something delightful in store for you, my darling turncoat."

Brett and Eden ran from the house and stopped to catch their breath on the sidewalk. Embla and Cillian stood in wait. Fresh blood dripped from their maws.

"You can't touch us! Remember? We're free to go!" Eden panted. The ghouls grinned garishly.

"Silly girl, you were free to leave … the house. We never agreed to a step further."

"Well … shit …" Eden said before Embla bit into her throat.

Cillian clamped his fangs into Brett's already mangled arm then snapped his neck when the whimpering got too distracting. Casting the emptied bodies of the ill-fated internet darlings aside, Embla and Cillian pricked their ears to the night sky.

"What am I hearing? Embla asked. "What *is* that?"

Cillian licked his fingers after wiping the excess gore from his face. "I think it's an accordion."

Jessie rode proudly down Main Street atop Sparklemane. His fingers lit up the accordion like electricity from a Tesla Coil as he played the theme song from *The Golden Girls.*

The shops and trees swayed like in the old cartoons as he passed. Flying saucers swooped overhead and dropped twinkling, radioactive confetti. Bigfoot folded his newspaper and uncrossed his legs at the coffee shop so he could encourage Jessie to keep going. But Jessie had no intention of stopping. He was going back to The Source, one way or the other—either by violent folkloric fuckery, or chemical brain liquification. Either way, he was ready.

Embla and Cillian made short time crossing town to find the cause of the music, and what they saw took them aback.

"Why is he walking like that?" Cillian asked as he watched Jessie awkwardly-yet-confidently ambled bowlegged. "Does he think he's riding a horse? Is he trying to defecate? And who is he shouting at?"

"He was with the one who had hallucinogens in his blood," Embla smiled. "Looks like you and I are in for a treat!" They rushed towards Jessie with eager fangs.

"They're coming, Jessie ..." Alan Sparklemane said solemnly.

"I know, friend. It's time I played my part."

"I wish I could do more to help."

"Hush, you've always been my bes—" Jessie's words were cut short by the pouncing ghouls.

The three fell in slow motion—in Jessie's estimation—and his accordion clattered on the pavement. Embla and Cillian drank greedily of the fallen hero, who slowly watched his unicorn friend disintegrate into a shimmering cloud of rainbow prisms. Jessie's fingers kept playing as though he still held his instrument. After several deeper draughts, his fingers finally stopped.

"Guh! My god! The—*mm*—the taste!" Cillian pulled his mouth free from the right side of Jessie's throat and attempted to compose himself. "It's like electricity!"

"Mmm … stronger than the one before …"

Embla wiped her mouth and licked her fingers. Cillian stared at her in awe with dilated pupils.

"What …?

"I see you. For the first time, I truly see you!"

"What madness are you spouting? The drugs haven't kicked in yet, have they?"

Embla pulled her hood down, revealing her long, flowing hair and smokey gray eyes of long ago.

"I'm—why are you staring?"

"Is this what Cicero saw the night he turned you?" Cillian asked in awe at Embla's perceived beauty. "The way the moonlight plays upon your golden locks, like a—"

"—Don't ruin the mood with mediocre poetry, child."

Embla said as she removed her cloak, revealing her suppleness. Cillian smiled and removed his as well. Embla ran her fingers across her companion's fair-haired chest then down, down until he gasped with delight. They lowered themselves onto the undulating, gasoline-puddle-colored lawn and began to kiss.

"I was jealous, you know," she said, uncharacteristically meek.

"Of what?" Cillian asked as he ran his swirling, snake-like fingers across her breasts.

"Of your youth. Of your *eyes.* They still retain some color, while mine have faded over time. Devoid of the life they once held."

"Nonsense! They glisten like stars in an endless night! Moonlight-dappled gems plucked from Eden's Garden."

"Don't spoil this …"

Across the street, Mitch Claremont watched the rutting ghouls from his window in a *good-lord-I-don't-want-to-see-this-but-I-can't-bring-myself-to-look-away* train wreck sort of way. He winced and groaned with each tonguing of their various gnarled body parts. He saw them the way they actually were: Two sinister creatures who had no business being naked out in the open.

"Mitch, what are you looking at?" His wife, Ellen, asked. "You know better than to look at the blood and guts. Remember what Doctor Morton said? We've got to stay disassociated from the violence, so we don't feel guilty and ruin it for everyone else."

"They're fornicating…" Mitch stated in disgusted reverence.

"What?"

"Two of the Benefactors, Ellen. They're … they're … *fucking.*" Mitch winced. Ellen swiftly moved to her husband's side and gasped.

"I didn't know they could, you know … make love. I'm putting the kettle on. And getting the binoculars."

Off Ellen went. Mitch just shook his head.

"I don't know if what they're making could be considered love, Ell. And why you'd want to see it closer is beyond me. Pour me a scotch on your way back, would you?"

"Neat? Two fingers?" Ellen shouted from the kitchen.

Mitch watched Embla mount Cillian and ride him like a nightmare.

"Better make it four."

Lee-Lee headbanged the sweet sting of sweat from her eyes. Bella and Mia were in the middle of their keyboard/guitar solo duel in the song "There Is No Title For This Song," and the energy was extraordinary.

Dax and Rafael kept the rhythm despite the chaos. Lee-Lee loved it when the band sounded like they knew what they were doing. They drove all the way from a show in Mechanicsburg, Pennsylvania to Commack, Long Island to play at The Nappy Dugout for around eight people, including staff. They were exhausted and borderline malnourished, but they didn't care. This was life in a rock-and-roll band. Or punk. Whatever they semi-agreed on that day. It was time for the last verse. Lee-Lee looked up at the mostly empty bar and sneered.

"Right hates left!
Left hates right!
We're all just cannon fodder for the brute!
Gnats flying 'round low watt

mediocre minds in suits!
Now what?
We watch the show like good little sheep!
Dance, puppets, dance!
Clap, children clap!
We're running out of soapboxes and
Tinfoil for our hats!
Let's start a fucking revolution
right after these messages!
Stay tuned!
Log in!
Can't you assholes just get along?
Stay numb!
Sell out!
There is no title to this song!"

The music pounded to a crescendo then stopped before the crash. Jessie struck his triangle.

"Thank you, um, this place! We're Grundle Busket … have a … night!"

Lee-Lee placed her hand over her brow to block the stage lighting and saw a row of red candles adorning the length of the bar top. The bar was empty—well, *extra* empty.

"We better get the hell out of here, guys …"

Lee-Lee turned to face the band, but they had been eviscerated. She recoiled and fell backwards off the stage and into the waiting arms of the three hooded fiends.

"Encore!" cheered one of them, then they fell upon Lee-Lee in a heap of fangs and impatient fingers.

Lee-Lee woke up on the large conference table in one of the back rooms, still wrapped in a blanket. Her shout was silent, parched. Dax stirred from his nap on an office chair from the sudden movement.

"You okay, Lee?"

"Everyone's dead, Dax." Lee-Lee shuddered. "We're next."

"Shut that shit right down, babe. We're safe in this office. Those fuckers already came through. No reason to come back, right? It's damn near morning and all we have to do is nothing."

The buzzing of the fluorescent lights added to the uneasiness Lee-Lee felt, but there was no way in hell they'd turn them off. Dax clambered onto the table next to Lee-Lee and held her.

"We get out of this, the first thing we do is call the number on that card. Maybe at a restaurant. I don't know about you, but that vending machine ain't cutting it."

"I could go for a Bingo-Bango burger…"

"I'm thinking, after all this unholy shit we've been through? We need a Pearly Gates Express Bucket from JFC."

"Ugh, I fucking hate Jesus Fried Chicken, Dax! Nothing but hateful hypocrites and bigots."

"I know, but like I said, after this? We need a place that'll 'Fry the hell out of it' like the slogan says."

They both shared a soft chuckle. Dax kissed her on the temple.

"See? Got your mind off of things for a second, didn't I?"

"Yeah," Lee-Lee admitted with a smile. "I'm sorry again for what I put you through, you know, after what happened. It wasn't fair. You—"

"—No more apologizing," Dax interjected then kissed her temple again. "Sun comes up, we get the van and peace the fuck out of this hell hole. Deal?"

"Deal."

Their lips met for the first time in a long while, and finally something that night felt right.

"Any idea where my aunt is?"

"I think I hear her yelling …" Dax said.

They quickly got off of the table and headed into the hallway. Aunt Gretta was banging on the sigil door with a fire extinguisher. Dax rushed to grab it.

"Whoa! Hold up!"

"Get your hands off me!" Aunt Gretta snarled.

Dax wrestled the extinguisher from her hands and backed away.

"What the hell is happening, Aunt Gretta?" Lee-Lee asked.

"Sam refuses to contact Lucas!" she sneered. "So, I thought I'd bust the door in so he's as much at risk of dismemberment as the rest of us!"

"You can't break through the door, Gretta," Sam sighed. "It's reinforced."

"What if I was the one hittin' it?" Dax chimed in. Lee-Lee was taken aback. "Or maybe try the shotgun you said was in the cruiser trunk?"

"Dax…" Lee-Lee put her hand on his arm and shook her head.

"I just want to know he's alright, Sam," Aunt Gretta said, her tone becoming sad. "I just want to hear his voice one more time."

"Gretta, we're damn near dawn! The cameras haven't picked up any movement for a long time. The Benefactors just might be gone."

"Then what's the harm in trying the radio?" Aunt Gretta asked.

"Because they might *not* be."

"Please, Sam. Just a quick hello."

"Hhhh … Jesus and Mary—Lucas—you sure know how to pick 'em. Fine, I'll—despite my better fucking judgement—hail him."

Cicero cradled Uncle Lucas in his arms. The

vampire held him firmly as his body completed the death throes, then brushed an errant wisp of hair from Lucas' sweat-dampened forehead.

"That wasn't so bad, was it?" Cicero smiled. "Believe me, child, it will only get worse from here. Savor those last gasps, seriously. This is something you will look back upon with bitter-sweet reverie. Momentarily, at least. I cannot stand betrayal. I cannot tolerate those who have the world at their fingertips yet cannot see beyond their wrists. I understand the treachery, I do. You've been a lackluster participant since your father died, and that—*incident*—with your brother. I'm sure that has soured you. I understand, child. However, in the grand scheme of immortality, one tends to toss potential repercussions into the nearest sepulcher."

"Talking to the dead?" Embla asked as she and Cillian entered the no-longer-safe room.

Cillian walked to the security cameras and stared entranced.

"For now, dearest. Say … you two have been quite busy, eh? I can smell the rut upon you both. And what's wrong with him? And *why* are you staring at your fingers? Oh, do *not* tell me you have dined on yet another drugged mortal and didn't think to include me!"

"Sorry, Cicero." Embla frowned then smiled then frowned then laughed.

Suddenly, the HAM radio squawked.

"Lord below!" Cillian shrieked and jumped from the electronics.

"Lucas! CQ, CQ. Lucas, you there? It's all good," Sam said.

"Lucas' brood must be at the police station," Cicero smiled. "The fool should have kept his mouth shut."

"Shall we?" Embla grinned.

"You two go on ahead. I'll be along forthwith."

Cicero nodded towards the door. The others bowed and rushed out with as much grace as their stoned legs would grant them. Cicero set Lucas on the carpet and walked to the hissing radio.

"Lucas?" Sam asked once again. Cicero lifted the microphone and pressed the red button.

"Thank you, Chief Harris," Cicero began with a soft chuckle. "We *do* so hate loose ends."

13

"Oh … oh *fuck* ... Oh fucking fuck!" Sam slammed the receiver down and banged on the sigil door twice. "You all need to bug out *now*! I told you that was a dumb-fucking idea!"

"Stop screaming, Sam! What did you hear?" Aunt Gretta added to the tension with her *I-have-no-more-time-for-your-drama* drama.

"Cicero knows you're here and he's coming! Dax, get the cruiser running, grab the shotgun and load it full of the special rounds in the bag in the trunk. We're not ready for this. We weren't *supposed* to be ready for this until the next time! Three years from now! This was supposed to be fact finding and exposure, not a god damned DEFCON one!"

"Ah … Chief?" Powell pointed to the front door, where Embla stood. Smiling. Waving.

"Get to the goddamn car!" Sam shouted as Embla tugged at the locked door.

"Oh … you've locked me out. How cheeky!" Embla laughed then ripped the door from its hinge. She entered the station then paused at the gore- soaked intake window and the mangled body beneath it. "Do you see this? That body is composed of slithering eels. Am I correct? You, new boy—what do you see?"

Powell approached the window with little hesitation, knowing that the longer he could stall the undead nightmare, the better the odds were of the others surviving.

"Are those eels?" Powell rubbed his chin. "Must be. You couldn't be wrong. Though, there are over eight hundred species of eel in the world. Do you know which ones we're looking at?"

"No … that doesn't seem right. Who are you again?"

"I'm the deputy …" Powell lied politely.

"I don't recall you … what is your name?"

"Michael Meline, ma'am," Powell pressed his fake ID to the window. "We met three years ago, after my father passed away while foiling a jewel runner heist. You called him pathetic for having such a weak constitution."

"That does sound like something I would say," Embla laughed. Suddenly, her attention snapped to the sound of Dax shouting.

"What's the fucking code for the door?"

"Shut up!" roared Sam. "Same code I already gave you! It's all the same code!"

"Oh! *There* they are!" Embla smiled. "The stragglers."

She stalked to the back area door and turned the knob. Despite being locked, she managed to snap the mechanism with little effort.

"God damn it!" Sam shouted as he rushed the sigil door.

Powell placed himself between the two.

"The fuck are you doing?"

"Something that doesn't feel right but has to happen for this whole thing to end," Powell said with undeniable guilt. "Open the door, we die, *and* they die. Keep it shut and we stand a chance to finish the plan. For the greater good."

"That's the shit I was fed by my dad who was fed that shit by *his* dad and so forth back to when this sham of a town was formed." Sam pushed the words through gritted teeth.

"Couple of hundred years of shit later and here we are." Powell looked to his dog Bukowski, who gave him no philosophical validation. "I hate everything about this, but we have to let it play out. I don't want to die in New Hampshire."

"Hurry the hell up, kids!" Harris pleaded.

"Hurry the hell up, Dax!" Lee-Lee agreed.

"All this yelling is *really* fucking helping!" Dax growled as his fingers scrambled across the keypad. "One … seven … six … one …" Dax tried the handle to no avail. "What the hell? That's the code!"

Embla kicked the other door into the hallway then poured herself in like an elegant, venomous reptile.

"You all look like scared rabbits!" Embla gasped. "How utterly perfect!"

"Hit enter!" Lee-Lee ordered then pushed it herself.

In Dax's defense, the button didn't register through his panic. He pulled the handle down as Embla rushed the corridor on unsteady legs. The door opened. The three practically fell into the garage and Dax slammed the door shut just as Embla reached out to claim them. Her impact boomed in the large space. Dax and Lee-Lee raced to the back of the garage. Dax pulled the tarp from the cruiser and unlocked its trunk. He then tossed Lee-Lee the keys.

"Fire this bitch up!" he yelled, and Lee-Lee did just that.

The engine rumbled, kicking black smoke at Dax who was busy loading the shotgun with the special rounds Chief Harris mentioned.

"This better fucking work!"

The whole precinct seemed to shake from Embla's blows, but the frame held. The door, on the other hand, began to buckle. Dax slid into the passenger's seat and handed Lee-Lee a tactical security flashlight. He then turned the flashlight fixed to the bottom of the shotgun on, filling the cabin with ultraviolet light. The upper left section of the door bent violently from the frame, giving Embla a place to grip.

"Get this goddamned thing moving, Lee!" Aunt Gretta cried as she opened the back door and got in. She was just about to close the cruiser door when her niece turned to her.

"What if we just use the lights? Sit here covered in UV until sunup?" Lee-Lee suggested. Aunt Gretta banged her palm on the metal mesh barrier between them.

"Because that hell-bitch will just flip the goddamn car until we're dead or throw us into the lake and laugh while we drown! Open the garage door and step-the-fuck-on-it!"

Lee-Lee frantically searched for a button that would open the garage door remotely. "There's no button!" she shouted as Embla bent the door open even more.

The vampire smiled as she saw the little rabbits tremble in their hutch.

"Look at these precious coneys!" Embla smiled. "Father had a recipe fit for a king, but I always preferred the meat less *dead* before I ate it. Could be why I was the one sold to slavery and not my siblings, now that I think on it …"

"I've always hated this bitch," Aunt Gretta

growled as she got out of the cruiser.

"Get in! What are you doing?" Lee-Lee shouted.

"Doing my part. I've given these pieces of undead shit too much. Family, happiness, peace, freedom—I know there's hypocrisy in what I'm saying, but we don't have time for clarity. Get the hell out of town and make lots of babies. Oh! And have your lawyer call our lawyer."

Aunt Gretta slammed the car door closed and hurried to the garage door panel. Embla managed by that time to nearly bend half the door down. The garage door made a rattling *chung-chung-chung* sound as it opened, slowly revealing a poised and prepared Cillian. He had prepared a poem.

"As the world below us gently sighs–
If we burned like stars
would you be content?
plummeting through
an Autumn sky
as the world below us
gently sighs
and draws near

oh, how stylish
such guttural beauty
dying the very same
way
we've lived:
untamed
and sudden."

"Hit this fool with the high beams!" Dax suggested as Lee-Lee hit the gas.

The lights came on, the tires squealed, Embla

tore the door down and rushed the vehicle, Aunt Gretta laughed as she listened to Cillian's burning flesh screams.

The cruiser struck the poet as all vehicles should. Cillian's face smashed onto the hood while his sternum was compacted by the ram bars. He held on despite the pain. Aunt Gretta trained her flashlight onto Embla, burning her hands as they instinctively covered her face. The vampire laughed as the searing pain coursed through her flesh like sunlight through a canopy. Embla slashed Aunt Gretta in a single fluid strike, tearing deep canyons into her face and upper body. The cruiser tore out of the garage and hit a hard right, pulling Cillian along. The headlights boiled and burned his face as he screamed. Embla watched the ashes and embers swirl into the night air like fireflies, and she paused at its exquisiteness. His howls of pain undulated across the avenue like a banner affixed to a biplane. Cillian clawed his way from the bumper to the hood and screeched at the escaping lovers with lungs full of hate and half of a face. His green eyes burned bright through bubbling, ashen flesh.

"I will devour your wretched souls!"

"Here's an appetizer, you Harvey Dent-looking motherfucker!"

Dax chambered a round and fired it through the windshield, sending Cillian—with his new crescent-moon-shaped head—to the concrete and under the wheels in a series of moist thuds. The glass showered the cabin, causing Lee-Lee to flinch and swerve into Cicero, who stood like an oak tree in the middle of the road.

"This. Ends. Now!" the ancient ghoul shouted.

The car struck him, yet he did not budge. Instead, the cruiser spun then flipped three times until coming to a rest on its roof. Lee-Lee hung upside down from her seatbelt. She spit some glass out and looked at Dax, who was crumpled on the ground.

"This sacrosanct mockery of a sacred pact has gone on long enough!"

"Dax! W-wake up!"

She reached her buckle with a shaky hand and managed to undo it after several attempts. She slumped to the ground and shook him. "Don't you fucking leave me in the middle of a set!"

"This … wasn't in the band rider …" Dax stirred. "Lilly … two things I have to say, then I want you to run like hell."

"You're running with me, baby—don't you fucking think otherwise."

Lee-Lee righted herself and located the flashlight. Her fingers fumbled for the "on" button.

"Ready to end this, rabbits?" Embla crouched down and smiled into the cabin.

"Don't I get some last words?" Dax shouted. "I got something to tell the love of my life before you rip my head off. That ok? They got manners where you come from, bitch?"

"Make it quick," Embla sneered, then rose to her feet.

"The Hades are you doing?" Cicero scowled. "Tie the loose ends up and let us depart!"

"Last words," Embla looked lovingly upon her maker.

He looked as regal as he did when he turned her in the monastery so many moons ago.

"You are resplendent tonight, my maker. And what is the harm of letting the sheep bleat one last time?"

"Lilly," Dax began as he maneuvered himself into a more functional position. "I love you—have always loved you. I will try my god-damnedest to find you in the next life. One without bullshit vampires in it, hopefully …" The two kissed. A decade of struggle and victory and stagnation blew into the air like fireflies. "Nothing matters until everything matters. Then you realize that everything matters until nothing does. Cherish it all regardless."

"I love you too," Lee-Lee said through her tears. "You should have written our lyrics. That was poignant AF."

"As Foretold?" Dax smiled and the two kissed again.

"As Foretold," she softly stated with a bittersweet smile.

"Look over my shoulder," Cicero ordered Embla. "Through your drug-addled eyes, what do you see?"

"I see …" Embla watched the vermilion glow of the morning slowly invade the mountaintops. "… release."

"You see damnation!" Cicero scolded as he clutched her throat. "Let us finish tying these last threads and seek refuge. *Now.*"

"Run, babe." Dax's smile turned into a wince as Embla ripped the door off and pulled him from the car.

Lee-Lee stifled her gasp. Embla held Dax by the throat and mused at his attempt to rack another shotgun round singlehandedly like they could in the movies. It wasn't to style. It was, instead, due to his left arm bones being emulsified by the crash.

"What is he trying to accomplish?" Cicero cocked his eyebrow.

"I think it's a sad attempt at being Jonathan Wayne," Embla laughed.

Dax sneered.

"James Edwards, bitch," he said, then smashed

the shotgun's butt into Cicero's face while maintaining his grip on the pump. The round chambered, and Dax drop-slid the gun down and caught it. "Look him up if you survive the—"

His words were cut short by Embla's tightened grip. Her other hand took hold of the barrel of the shotgun.

"I will. Or perhaps you could—"

Embla's words were cut short by a shotgun round to the thigh, causing her to buckle ever so slightly. The meat of her left thigh stung and singed but was too far evolved to succumb to the attack. She sucked in the pain like a masochist then looked into Dax's eyes.

"Oooh, my lovely lamb. That actually made me *feel* something."

"Give me that!" Cicero easily plucked the shotgun from Dax's hand and sniffed the smoky barrel. "Salt and … silver? Harris gave you this, did he? And the modified vehicle? I will pay him a visit tomorrow night and rectify this whole cock-up of a tithing."

"I'm no snitch, you pasty-assed, Spirit-Halloween-clearance-bin looking motherfucker," Dax said defiantly.

Embla sunk her fangs into his neck and held him tight. The entry points gushed in the millisecond it took for the vampire to seal her lips around the wound. Cicero saw the evanescent spurt and was so aroused that he couldn't help but join in.

As they fed, Lee-Lee ran as fast as her shaky legs could carry her. She slid-sprinted across the dew-dappled field of Pacton Park, and past the gazebo that historically touted politicians, poets, playwrights, and a slew of musicians on their way up or down from success. She used to run this path in her childhood. She knew that just beyond the gazebo was the hill that not only caused many a drunken plummet, but was also the quickest route to the docks. Lee-Lee saw the dawn lurking like a zombie at the tip of the tree line and knew that the lake was her best bet. She tucked and rolled like the local kids used to shout as they each took turns down the hill.

"Maker," Embla said after the sickening pluck of her lips from Dax's neck. "Your loose end."

She saw the irradiated glow of the sun rising like a fleet of pustulous cherubim.

"Find shelter. We will tend to our retribution upon nightfall. Oh, and do save me some of this one, will you?"

Cicero wiped his mouth then sped off in a blur. In a matter of seconds, the ancient vampire stood at the pier where Lee-Lee fought with the mooring of a rowboat. She clenched the flashlight in crook of her left armpit while her trembling fingers attempted to work the knot from the mooring cleat.

"Child, it is over. Come to me and we shall set this right. You have run a truly respectable campaign, but it has ended. The outcome was never in question, you see. I do not lose. The Goddess Nox had granted me the gift of—"

"—You mean Nyx?" Lee-Lee laughed. "The Romans really didn't give much effort in ripping religions off the way the Christians did. Easter notwithstanding. Or Yule …"

"I offer you immortality, and yet you *mock* me, child?" Cicero set a wary foot onto the dock. The dawn was a mere whisper away, yet his hubris couldn't allow Lee-Lee to live. "I have seen empires rise and crumble, witnessed peasants become kings and kings become corpses. I've danced upon sanguine-soaked battlefields in the dazzling glow of Mother Moon. Pain and despair will grace your existence never again. Come … take my hand and live forever."

"I'm pretty sure those aren't the lyrics to 'Sympathy for the Devil'."

Lee-Lee pressed the flashlight's button and trained it on Cicero. The ultraviolet light singed his face. He pulled his hood closer to his skin and hissed.

"Oh look, pain has graced your existence. Fuck you. Fuck immortality. And fuck your ancient—*dead*—whore of a mother."

"Impudent bitch!" Cicero roared and began his march down the dock when Powell's drone swooped close to his face.

The wind from the propellers caused the cloak's hood to flap back, allowing Lee-Lee a good shot for the flashlight. Cicero recoiled with a shriek. The sun was now cresting the tree lines and mountaintops, but the blighted town of Pacton was still coiled in darkness. Cicero smashed the drone to the ground and covered himself from the flashlight's beam. Lee-Lee had placed the flashlight on top of a mooring post and was already rowing like mad.

She paused. Both of her middle fingers pointed high above her head. It wasn't out of a sense of victory, but out of spite. Defiance. Cicero watched her stand strong on the bobbing rowboat and he seethed. The sun rays crept slowly through the trees like a stalking beast. Lee-Lee thought of her bandmates, her family, her lover—their unborn child, the life they could have had—and smiled through the tears.

"I never lose!" Cicero roared.

"You just did, dick skin!" She laughed. "I'm gonna tell everyone about you sick fuckers! You'll be hunted down, and the world will be better because of it. You're just old money parasites. That's it. You never did anything worth a damn—just leeched off the rest of us. But thanks for the inspiration! My next band's gonna be called Impudent Bit—"

She felt the impact in her sternum before she felt the pain. Her knees buckled. Her breath cut short and was unable to return. Instinctively, her fingers probed the wound and found a portion of the blood-slick, flickering flashlight. Blood sputtered from her mouth. She could no longer see her adversary, only the gilded town of her youth that had done wrong to so many. Lee-Lee felt the burning fade like a memory as the bittersweet autumnal sun caressed her skin.

Epilogue

I put on a Pacton PD windbreaker and open the rear door of the cruiser that the Chief parked behind the station. Bukowski gets in back, then I buckle in. I hope the ruse works. Otherwise, I'll be just another black bag on its way to an acid barrel. Sam gets in, starts the engine, then hangs his head.

"What is it?" I ask, nervous enough already.

"If I can't get you out, it's all for nothing. All the death, corruption, and … everything. It all goes unanswered."

"Better get me out then."

"Heh, yeah." Sam puts the cruiser in gear, and we make a left out of the lot. "You good with leaving your gear in the precinct?"

"Yeah," I nod. "The hard drives and memory cards are on me. Everything else is replaceable."

We pass a team of people in yellow hazmat suits pulling equipment from a large van. Looks to be pressure washers. They all stop and stare at us. Sam makes a Han Solo salute with his right hand as if this is just what we were supposed to be doing. Just two cops patrolling the town after a massive, pre-determined—

and authorized—massacre. We creep past the Kelly house, which according to my notes, was the venue of a cult recruitment by a serial scammer. What the hell is a Dukehouse? Another team in hazmat suits pulls black bag after black bag from the house. One stops hosing blood and bits of skull from the sidewalk to study us. This time I'm the one waving. I get none in return. The car stops, and I hear Sam breathe sharply through his nose. I see what he's looking at, a charred body—mostly ash and smoke—nailed to the East-facing roof of the Allore house like a scarecrow. We both know who it is.

"That's my fault," Sam rubs his face with both hands. "I never should have radioed Lucas."

"While that's true, they probably would have done that to him regardless. Though—in all honesty—you did put everyone at risk by doing that. Not that it matters, since they all died anyway."

"You are zero fucking help," Sam says.

"I'm not here for your conscience, I'm here to end a nightmare. Try to, at least."

"The fact that you put yourself at so much risk is a testament to your—"

"—Save the blowjob for after we're a town over. Don't mistake what I'm doing as friendship, Chief. Once this shit is exposed, you'll be just as damned as everyone else despite the plot to end it. You can't escape the repercussions by the law or by monsters."

I regret saying that so soon. I'm concerned Sam will stop the car and blow my brains out. Sweep me under the Rug of Centuries, so to speak. Sometimes I get too sanctimonious for my own good, but he chuckles softly and turns the car towards a small, dirt road in the tree line.

"I know. I made peace with that when I called

you. Like I told you on the phone that day, just because my great grandfather did it, my grandfather did it, my father did it, and even I did it, doesn't mean I have to keep doing it."

The tires spit rocks like an old-timey saloon patron into a spittoon as we pothole-shimmy the suspension down the path. Sam tells me it's not on the map, just a path that the locals know. My theory is if the locals—any of them—know, then there's a good chance the bastards-that-be do too. My theory proves correct as we approach a couple of sawhorses at the end of the path festooned with more hazmat minions. I notice one of them has an AR.15 pistol with a horizontal barrel grip attachment (vertical is a felony, just FYI) close to his hip. Not terribly subtle, but it makes sense for the off-beaten path. One does not use this route by accident. Hazmat holds his hand up for us to stop. That's when I also notice the two rottweilers.

"Here's where we find out how good we can act." Sam clears his throat as he slows the car down. "You got your ID ri—" I cut him off with it, ready and visible. The cruiser crawls to a painful, bobbing stop. We roll the windows down.

"This is unlike you, Harris," Hazmat number one says.

"Something new, hired goon … sorry, you all look the same."

"Who the fuck is that?" HG1 asks, blatantly rubbing his finger along his pistol.

"Michael Meline, sir." I hand my ID over without hesitation. "Chief's teaching me the ropes of what comes after … you know. Legacy and all that."

I realize that HG2 has been walking the large dog around the car. Bukowski presses his face to the window and growls. He sometimes reminds me a lot of his previous owner, Doyle, though not enough for me to disown him outright. The dogs growl, and that's a good thing. Distractions are useful when it comes to smuggling.

"Shut your dog up," HG1 orders.

Now's the moment of make-or-break at the crossroads of Fuck Around Road and Find Out Lane. I choose to be bold like my pup and his previous owner.

"Shut *your* fucking dog up," I say, much to Sam's shock.

"Pardon?" HG1 chuckles and caresses his thumb on the AR's safety. Now's the moment.

"We work for the Benefactors, and you work for us. How, you ask? Because we give them bodies, they give us money, and most importantly, *we* are the ones who renew your contract every time we need a janitor, so, let's do the math …"

I pretend to count on my fingers and carry invisible numbers in ethereal equations. HG1 and 2 side-eye each other. Now's the time to crank the pressure.

"You boys ever heard of *Better Call Barnabas*?" I can actually hear their assholes suck in the appropriate part of their suits.

"You know about those dipshits?" HG1 asks.

"Fuck those pussies!" HG2 grunts.

"Not without reason and consent," I state and attempt to exit the vehicle turning to the next notch on the pressure dial.

HG1 flips off the safety and Sam puts a sweaty hand on my arm.

"Fuck are you doing, man?"

"Due diligence," I reply softly then turn my attention back to the goons. "Look, guys, I'm just doing my part to make sure Chief Harris—*when it's time*—leaves this monster of a lucrative arrangement in capable hands. And I have those hands. You plan on giving me a reason to look into alternatives, I will. Otherwise, give me my ID back, and take your fucking finger off that trigger, and allow us to hit the Bingo Bango Burger before they run out of deliciously seasoned, breakfast PigBird sliders. You want a couple? We can bring you back a couple."

"N-no …" HG1 stammers as he tries to spin a few plates.

"That's the genetically engineered pig and chicken meat shit I heard about?" HG2 chimes in.

I smile and give a thumbs up.

"Yup! 'The Breakfast Beast', copyright symbol or whatever."

"I'll take one with a medium coffee with twelve sugars and soy milk." HG2 nods.

"And you?" I ask HG1, who is still spinning plates.

I can tell that his entire being is ping-ponging between integrity and *I don't get paid enough for this shit.*

"A … coffee, I guess? Black, no sugar?"

Got him.

"Like a *real* man," I nod. "You got it."

HG1 nods and pulls the sawhorse to the side. We continue on, leaving the death-drenched New England town behind. Sam is breathing heavily, like a kid who's sitting on a bench outside the principal's office.

"You were way off script," he says between gulps of oxygenated fear.

"Since there wasn't one, I figure I wasn't."

"The plan was to shut the hell up and—"

"—get shot in the face. No, thanks. My way got us across town lines. Your job is to get those bootlickers their fast-food order after you drop me off."

"Yeah, except ..." Sam taps the steering wheel nervously. "I come back without you, they'll shoot *me* in the face."

"Calculated risk of being a mass murder-enabler with a conscience. You got me out here for a reason—had my life on the line for a reason. I did and will do my part. Don't fuck it up on your end of the deal."

After fifteen minutes of tense silence, we pull into the Bingo Bango parking lot and park next to my Winnebago. Bukowski barks excitedly at the prospect of seeing his bed and stuffed Scooby Doo BFF/fuck buddy plushie. Again, not originally my dog. He was definitely a rescue.

"Well ... I guess this is it." Sam holds his hand out for a shake. I scoff and point at the restaurant.

"You owe me a breakfast—*us* a breakfast."

I nod to Bukowski who is an avid proprietor of greasy spoons.

"Sure." Sam turns the car off and sighs. "I got at least until nightfall to get my shit together."

"The shit you *had* together was the plan. I'm the only thing moving it forward from this point. You really want to make a difference? Come with me as a main witness. You'll add credibility to the already damning evidence. I might need a few dozen lie detector tests from you in order to add the slightest bit of credence against this whole thing being a guerilla-style horror flick, though."

I exit the cruiser and let the dog out from the back. Sam pauses, then fires the vehicle back up.

"They'll be after me by sunset. That's just the way it's always been. You won't be safe if I'm with you. Take what you have, write what you can—maybe we'll be able to bring a few hundred years of tradition to an end. Take care of yourself, Parker. Thanks for actually giving this a shot."

Sam puts the cruiser in gear then takes off. I salute him for some reason. For some other reason, I have a strong feeling that we'll succeed in our mission. I suppose it feels strange due to the likelihood. Hope and doubt and angst and vindication crash like a typhoon between the ocean of my mind and the shore of my bitter understanding of the world. I honestly don't know what to believe, but I signed up for the job and I'll see it through.

I just hope that legacy, history, old money, and inconvenience doesn't once again stifle the truth. As damning as the evidence may be, I wouldn't bet a dime on it causing any real impact. Why would this be different from any other atrocity? Just another fake-news conspiracy, feeding the systems in place that taint truth, cause derision, and would make this nightmare just another American bloodsucker story. Still, I have to try. I made a pact after all ...

The burning in Dax's stomach is like no craving ever felt by a mortal. Every blood vessel in his body throbs like gout. The town of Pacton is still in quarantine protocol, yet the noise is a kaleidoscopic cavalcade of sensory overload. It is night. He sees iridescent eyes twinkling in the shadows. The hunger is everything. He can't help but scream.

GRUNDLE BUSKET

ON TOUR NOW!

HONEY SLUDGE
CITIZEN SQUATCH
FALUMPTUTIOUS
GRUNDLE BUSKET
NO PARKING
LIVE AT THE
AX GRINDER
$5
TUESDAY
11/02
8pm

SLUG WEEKEND

MULLET
HORSE.

GRUNDEL BUSKET

09/21 @7pm

SHOEHORN EMPORIUM

MARKY MOON PRESENTS:

VELVETTE UNDERPANT

GRUNDLE BUSKET

SEPT. 24TH 9PM $5 21 & OVER

HOGGZ LIVE MUSIC SHOWCASE

"CRANKIN' IT SINCE 1972"

About the Author

Peter Hammarberg is the lovable weirdo behind Gonzo-Horror novella *Gravenfrost*, and Sci-Fi adventure epic *Antillia: The Order of The Lucifuge* book one. His work has been hailed as a tour de force of literary excellence, subversive, crass, and wildly entertaining. He was born and raised on Long Island, New York, but now resides in the North Country of New Hampshire. His mother swears he was a normal pregnancy.

For more, check out: peterhammarberg.com

Suggested Listening

Kreeps:
"Skull Beneath the Smile"
"I Wanna Kill, Kill, Kill (Alright!)"
"I'm Losing All My Dreams"
"Hiding From the Sun"
"The Hunger (Blood In My Mouth)"

Type O Negative:
"All Hallows Eve"
"Everyone I Love Is Dead"
"Bloody Kisses (A Death in the Family)"

Peculiar Pretzelmen:
"Bang the Drum"
"Little Death"
"The Dead Hate the Living"
"Dirty Susan"

Ministry:
"Everyday Is Like Halloween"
"Scare Crow"

Twin Temple:
"Let's Have A Satanic Orgy"

Dommin:
"Without End"

The 69 Eyes:
"I Love The Darkness in You"

Leonard Cohen:
"You Want It Darker"

The Birthday Massacre:
"Midnight"
"Under Your Spell"
"Sleepwalking"

Nine Inch Nails:
"The Hand That Feeds You"

Nostalghia:
"Once I Was Beautiful"

K.Flay:
"Blood In The Cut"

King Dude:
"My Mother Was The Moon"
"Ain't No Graves (featuring Osi And The Jupiter)"

Whiskey Shivers:
"Graves"

The Wanton Bishops:
"Sleep With the Lights On"

Cemetery Skyline:
"The Coldest Heart"
"When Silence Speaks"

Dead Man's Bones:
"Lose Your Soul"

PJ Harvey, Thom Yorke:
"This Mess We're In"

Swans:
"Killing For Company"
"What Is This?"

*Open Spotify search, click the camera in the upper right-hand corner and scan this code to bring you to the playlist.

www.ingramcontent.com/pod-product-compliance
Lightning Source LLC
La Vergne TN
LVHW010923110826
845149LV00013B/2454

* 9 7 8 0 9 9 0 8 3 9 7 3 6 *